THE JEW CAR

THE
SEAGULL
LIBRARY OF
GERMAN
LITERATURE

FRANZ FÜHMANN

THE JEW CAR

Fourteen Days from Two Decades

TRANSLATED BY ISABEL FARGO COLE

LONDON NEW YORK CALCUTTA

This publication was supported by a grant
from the Goethe-Institut India

Seagull Books, 2019

© Franz Fühmann, *Autorisierte Werkausgabe in 8 Bänden*. Band 3:
Das Judenauto: Vierzehn Tage aus zwei Jahrzehnten. Hinstorff Verlag
GmbH, Rostock 1993, S. 9–172.

First published by Seagull Books in English translation in 2013

ISBN 978 0 8574 2 717 5

British Library Cataloguing-in-Publication Data
A catalogue record for this book is available from the British Library

Typeset by Seagull Books, Calcutta, India
Printed and bound by WordsWorth India, New Delhi, India

CONTENTS

THE JEW CAR

1929, The Great Depression

How deep down does recollection reach? A warm green appears as my memory's earliest image, the green of a tiled stove, its cornice apparently circled by the frieze of a gypsy camp, but that I know only from my mother's stories; no mental effort can recover this image. The green, though, has remained, a warm wine-bottle hue with a dull sheen, and whenever I call up this green, I feel myself floating in the air above the floorboards: Father had to hold me up, Mother said, to see the gypsies, as a two-year-old tot.

Then in my memory comes something soft and white that I had to sit still on for an endlessly long time, staring up into a black thing, cranked up and down,* and then an elderbush den with a

---

* In 1966 the German writer Uwe Johnson, working as an editor for Harcourt, Brace and World in New York, included *Das Judenauto* in a German-language anthology for learners. He asked Franz Fühmann for explanations of several passages. Here Fühmann wrote: 'Dear Mr Johnson, though just a few years younger than I, you must be one of the fortunate ones who no longer had to suffer this childhood martyrdom, forced

bench and a man on the bench who smelt of adventure and let me ride on his knee and stuck in my mouth a piece of luscious sweet sausage I chewed greedily, and this memory comes with a cry and a storm that snatched man and arbour away from me, whirling them into the void. Of course it was no storm gust, it was my mother's arm that snatched me from the green den, and the cry was her cry of alarm: the man whose knee had rocked me was a village laughing stock, a once-wealthy farmer, down on his luck, who staggered bandy-legged through the villages, begging for bread and schnapps; and the smell of wild adventure was the spirits on his breath; and the sausage was refuse from the horse butcher. Yet it must have been splendid to ride on his knee: it is the first image I still see quite clearly before me, and I was three years old at the time.

From then on the images come thick and fast: the mountains, the forest, the well, the house, the brook and the meadow; the quarry whose grottoes housed the sprites I invented; toads; hornets; the

---

to sit for a hundred thousand hours with an unwavering friendly smile on a polar bear skin and stare into a black box from which, supposedly, a little bird would appear, while a man draped in a black cloth constantly fiddled around behind the black box, moving it up and down—and that, as I said, a hundred thousand hours long.' (3 July 1967)

screech of the owl; the rowan-lined avenue outside the grey factory; the fair with its smell of nougat and the hurdy-gurdy clamour of the barkers; and finally the school with its whitewashed corridor, always dark despite the tall windows, down which, from all the classrooms, human fear crept like a wisp of fog. I have forgotten the teachers' faces; all I see is two slitted grey eyes above a long knife-sharp nose and a bamboo cane notched with rings; and the faces of my schoolmates too have faded and blurred but for one brown-eyed girl with a narrow, barely curved mouth and a high brow beneath short, fair hair: the face before whose eyes you first cast down your own, bewildered by an enigmatic power, is not one you forget, whatever bitter things came afterwards . . .

One summer morning in 1931, when I was nine years old, the class gossip, Gudrun K., black-braided, and garrulous as a pond full of frogs, burst into the classroom just a few minutes before the bell, as always, with her cry of 'Everyone, everyone, have you heard!' She panted as she yelled, and waved her arms round wildly; her breath came fast but she went on yelling, 'Everyone, everyone!' yelling and gasping for breath. As always the girls went rushing up to her, thronging her like a swarm of bees its queen, but we boys paid little heed to the fuss she was making; far too often she'd trumpeted some sensation that turned out to be a trifle.

And so we went on with our business; as we discussed the latest adventures of our idol Tom Shark,* Karli, our ringleader, showed us how to dispatch the deadliest wolfhound in a jiffy, Shark-style—thrust your hand down its maw, where the teeth are the sharpest, grab the upper jaw, yank down the lower jaw, wrench the skull round and kick the beast in the larynx—we heard a shrill scream from the throng of girls. 'Eeeew, how ghastly!' one of the girls had cried, a needle-keen squealing *eee* of panic fear. We whirled round and saw the girl standing with her hand raised to her gaping mouth and naked fright in her eyes, and the group of girls stood cringing. 'And then they mix the blood with pastry flour and bake it into bread!' we heard Gudrun blurt out, and we saw the girls shudder. 'What's this rubbish you're talking?' Karli shouted. The girls didn't hear. Reluctantly, we drew closer. 'And then they eat it?' one of them

---

* 'Perhaps he was a hero peculiar to German-Bohemian youth but he *was* this hero, he, by no means Tom Mix, whom we hardly knew at all. . . . he was German (what else, when he solved the most insanely hard cases) . . . and suffered from the flu each spring and fall . . . but it was then, as, sweating and sputtering, a towel over his head, he inhaled chamomile vapours, that the most interesting cases descended upon him and he solved them with a stuffed-up nose. He was always called in when the world's elite detectives had failed miserably and were at their wits' end, yet he was extremely modest and reluctant to speak of himself and his deeds.' (Fühmann to Johnson, 13 October 1966)

asked hoarsely. 'They eat it on their feast day, they all gather at midnight and light candles, and they say a magic spell and then they eat it!' Gudrun affirmed with panting fervour. Her eyes were glowing. 'What kind of magic spell?' asked Karli and laughed, but his laughter sounded fake. A strange fear seized me. 'Go on, tell us!' I hollered at Gudrun, and the other boys hollered too, and we thronged round the girls thronging Gudrun, and hastily, nearly yelling out the words, Gudrun repeated her story. A Jew car, she spluttered, had appeared in the mountains, driving in the evenings along the lonely country roads to snatch little girls and slaughter them and bake magic bread from their blood; it was a yellow car, all yellow, she said, her mouth and eyes screwed up with horror: a yellow car, all yellow, with four Jews inside, four swarthy, murderous Jews with long knives, and all the knives were bloody, and blood was dripping from the running board, people had seen it clear as day, and they'd slaughtered four girls so far, two from Witkowitz and two from Böhmisch-Krumma; they'd hung them by the feet and cut off their heads and drained the blood into vats, and we were piled on top of one another in a shrieking, quaking clump of fright, and Gudrun's shrill owl's voice was louder than our fear, avidly swearing, though no one doubted her story, that all of this was really true, she'd seen the Jew car herself. If she'd gone to

Böhmisch-Krumma yesterday to distribute piece-work, she'd have seen the Jew car with her very own eyes: yellow, all yellow, and the blood dripping from the running board, and I stared at Gudrun's red face and thought admiringly that she'd been awfully lucky not to get slaughtered, without a doubt in my mind about the Jew car driving through the fields and catching little girls.

I had never seen a Jew, but I'd learnt a lot about them from the grown-ups' conversations. They all had hooked noses and black hair and all the bad things in the world were their fault: they used dirty tricks to fleece honest people and they'd started the Depression that threatened to ruin my father's pharmacy; they took away the farmers' cattle and corn and bought up grain from all over, poured spirits over it and dumped it into the sea to make the Germans starve, because they hated us Germans beyond all reason and wanted to exterminate us all—so why shouldn't they lurk on country roads in a yellow car to snatch German girls and slaughter them? No, there was no doubt in my mind that the Jew car existed, and even the words of the teacher, who meanwhile had entered the classroom and pooh-poohed the shouting mouths' news of the Jew car, did nothing to alter my belief. I believed in the Jew car; I saw it drive, yellow, all yellow, between grainfield and grainfield, four swarthy Jews with long pointed knives,

and suddenly I saw the car stop and two of the
Jews bounded towards the grainfield by which a
brown-eyed girl sat weaving a crown of blue corncockles, and the Jews, knives between their teeth,
grabbed the girl and dragged her to the car, and
the girl cried out and I heard her cry and I was in
heaven, for it was my name she cried. She cried
my name loud and frantic; I searched for my Colt
but couldn't find it, and so I lunged bare-handed
out of my secret passageway and hurled myself at
the Jews. I dashed the first to the ground with a
blow to the chin; the second Jew, already lifting
the girl to bundle her into the car, I felled with a
chop to the neck; the Jew at the wheel stepped on
the gas and the car shot towards me, but of course
I was prepared and dodged to the side; the car
shot past, I leapt onto the back, smashed the roof
with a blow of my fist, wrenched the knife from
the lunging hand of the Jew next to the driver,
threw him out of the car, overpowered the Jew at
the wheel, slammed on the brakes, jumped out
and saw the girl lying in a swoon in the grass by
the grainfield, and I saw her face lying motionless
before me in the grass and suddenly all I saw was
her face: brown eyes, a narrow, barely curved
mouth and a high brow beneath short, fair hair,
and I saw cheeks and eyes and lips and brow and
hair and I felt that this face had always been veiled
and I saw it for the first time bare. Abashed, I

wanted to look away and couldn't and bent over the girl who lay motionless in the grass and touched, barely brushed her cheek with my hand, and I turned flaming hot, and suddenly my hand burnt: a sudden sting; my name thundered in my ear, I started awake and the teacher brought the ruler down on the back of my hand again. 'Two hours' detention,' he huffed, 'I'll teach you to sleep in school!' The class laughed. The teacher struck a third time; my hand swelled up, but I clenched my teeth: two rows in front of me sat the girl whose face I had seen in the grass, and I thought that only she wouldn't laugh at me. 'Sleeping in school—does the lad think his desk is a bed?' The teacher said it as a joke, and the class roared with laughter. I knew she would never laugh at me. 'Quiet!' yelled the teacher. The laughter ebbed. The welts on my hand turned blue.

After staying for detention I didn't dare go home; I walked slowly up the village street, casting about for a good excuse, and finally thought of telling my parents I'd been looking for the Jew car. So as to approach my house from the fields rather than the main road, I turned onto a dirt road, towards the mountains: grainfields to the right and meadows to the left, and grain and grass swayed above my head. I forgot detention and forgot the Jew car; I saw the girl's face in the rippling grass, and in the grain I saw her fair hair. The meadow's scent dazed the senses; the bellflowers' swelling flesh bobbed blue at chest height; the thyme sent out wild waves of stupefying scent; swarms of wasps hummed fiercely; and by the blue corncockles the poppies glowed, scorching poison, in the hottest of reds. The wasps buzzed wildly about my face, the sun steamed, the crickets shrieked a mad message at me, large birds shot up from the grain, by the corncockles the poppies blazed menacingly, and I was bewildered; till then I had stood innocently amid Nature like one of its creatures, a dragonfly or a walking blade of grass, but now it seemed to thrust me away, and a rift opened up between me and the surrounding world. No longer was I earth and no longer grass and tree and beast; the crickets shrieked, making me think of how they rub their wings together when they chirp, and suddenly that seemed obscene, and suddenly everything was changed, as though seen for the first time: the ears of grain rattled in the wind, grass clove to grass, the poppies glowed, a mouth, a thousand mouths of the earth, the thyme seethed bitter fumes, and I felt my body like an alien thing, a thing that was not I; I trembled and ran my nails over the skin of my chest and plucked at it; I wanted to scream and could only moan; I had utterly lost my bearings, when, pushing grain and grass aside, a brown car came slowly down the road.

Spotting it, I flinched as though caught in a criminal act; I snatched my hands away from my chest, and the blood shot to my head. I struggled to collect my thoughts. A car; how did a car get here? I stammered to myself, and suddenly I realized: the Jew car! A shudder ran through me; I stood transfixed. At first I'd thought I'd seen a brown car; now that I looked a second time, dismayed and goaded by a ghoulish curiosity, I saw that it was more yellow than brown, actually yellow, all yellow, a lurid yellow hue, and though at first I'd seen only three people inside, I must have seen wrong, or maybe one had ducked, surely one had ducked, there were four of them in the car and one of them had ducked to hurl himself at me, and at that I felt mortal fear. Mortal fear; my heart had stopped beating, I had never noticed its beats but now that it had stopped I felt it: a dead ache in my flesh, an empty space that convulsed and sucked out my life. I stood transfixed and stared at the car and the car came slowly down the road, a yellow car, all yellow, coming towards me, and then, as though someone had set machinery in motion, my heart began beating again, and now it was racing, and my thoughts raced helter-skelter: scream, run away, hide amid the grain, leap into the grass, but in the nick of time it occurred to me that I mustn't arouse suspicion and show that I knew it was the Jew car, and so, wracked with dread, I walked with

measured stride down the lane, with measured
stride before the crawling car, freezing cold while
the sweat ran from my brow, and I walked like that
for close to an hour, though it was only a few steps
to the village. My knees trembled; already about
to keel over, I heard a voice from the car like the
crack of a whip, accosting or commanding, and
everything went black before my eyes; all I felt was
my legs running, taking me with them; I saw and
heard no more and ran and screamed, and not till
the middle of the village street, with houses and
people round me, did I dare to look about, gasping,
and see that the Jew car had vanished without a
trace.

Of course I told my classmates the next morning
that the Jew car had chased me for hours and
almost caught up with me, and I'd escaped only by
zigzagging wildly, and I described the Jew car, yellow, all yellow, carrying four Jews waving bloody
knives, and I wasn't lying, because I'd seen it
all myself. My classmates listened breathlessly,
thronging me with admiring and envious gazes; I
was their hero and could have taken Karli's place
now as ringleader but I didn't want that, I wanted
only one gaze and yet I didn't dare to seek it. Then
the teacher came; we shouted the monstrous news
in his face; feverishly, I described what I'd experienced, and the teacher asked the time and place

and circumstances, and I was able to give all the details, no bluffs or contradictions, nothing but irrefutable facts: the yellow car, all yellow, its four swarthy occupants, the knives, the blood on the running board, the country road, the command to snatch me, my flight, the pursuit, and the class listened breathlessly, and the girl with the short, fair hair raised her hand, and now I dared to look her in the face, and she half-turned at her desk and looked at me and smiled, and my heart floated off. I was in heaven; I heard the crickets shriek and saw the poppies glow and smelt the scent of thyme, but all that no longer bewildered me, the world was whole again and I was a hero, escaped from the Jew car, and the girl looked at me and smiled and said in her calm, deliberate voice that yesterday her uncle had come to visit with two friends; they'd come in a car, she said slowly, and the word 'car' pierced my brain like an arrow; they'd come in a brown car, she said, and at the teacher's hasty question she said that they'd driven down the same road at the same time I claimed to have seen the Jew car, and her uncle had asked directions of a boy at the edge of the meadow, and the boy had run off screaming, and she ran her tongue over her thin lips and said, very slowly, that the boy by the road had worn green lederhosen just like mine, looking at me with a friendly smile, and I felt that everyone was looking at me and I felt their gazes buzzing fierce as wasps, swarms of wasps over bushes of thyme, and the girl smiled with the calm cruelty of which only children are capable, and when a voice bawled out from inside me that the silly goose was off her head, it was the Jew car, yellow, all yellow, and four swarthy Jews inside with bloody knives, I heard her calm voice as though from another world say through my bawling that she herself had seen me run from the car. She said it quite calmly, and I heard my bawling break off; I closed my eyes, there was a deathly silence, and suddenly I heard a laugh, a needle-keen, tittering, little girl's laugh as shrill as crickets chirping, and then a wave of laughter surged through the room and washed me away. I bolted out of the classroom and ran to the toilet and locked the door behind me; tears burst from my eyes, for a time I stood stunned in the caustic chlorine smell, empty of thoughts, and stared at the black-tarred, stinking wall and suddenly I knew: it was their fault! It was their fault, theirs and theirs alone; they'd done all the bad things in the world, they'd ruined my father's business, they'd created the Depression and dumped the wheat in the sea, they used dirty tricks to fleece honest people, and they'd played one of their dirty, rotten tricks to make a fool of me in front of the class: everything was their fault, them and no one but them! I gnashed my teeth: it was their fault! I wailed out their name; I pressed my fists to my eyes and stood in the black-tarred, chlorine-reeking boy's room and screamed their name: 'Jews!' I screamed, and again: 'Jews', and just the sound of it: 'Jews, Jews!' and I stood wailing in the toilet stall and screamed Jews Jews Jews Jews, and then I threw up. Jews. It was their fault. Jews. I retched and clenched my fists. Jews. Jews Jews Jews Jews. It was their fault. I hated them.

PRAYERS TO SAINT MICHAEL

12 February 1934, Workers' Uprising in Vienna

Two years later that scene was long since forgotten.
I had finished the five years of elementary school
in my home town and at the age of ten had become
a newly fledged pupil at Kalksburg by Vienna, a
Jesuit boarding school for the Catholic elite of central and southeastern Europe. A benefactor of my
father, Count H, himself a former Kalksburg pupil,
had smoothed the path, no easy one for sons of the
bourgeoisie. In mid-September 1932, I had taken
the train there with my father; hesitantly, I entered
the enormous school building that was like a
streetless white city and stood in a corridor that
must have been half a mile long, lit by high windows, where black-habited monks passed in the
distance with barely perceptible footsteps. The
corridor seemed a thousand times longer than the
corridor of my school back home, itself so long that
you felt lost in it, and this one was as high as a
church nave, its walls panelled in dark wood to
head height, and above the brown wood, between
window and window and door and door, hung

paintings of saints and battles. The corridor was silent as a grave; the monks glided without a sound, as though on rails. Hesitantly we entered; our steps echoed; we walked on tiptoe. A leather-covered door opened and a monk came out; my father approached him with a deep bow at which the monk nodded slightly; the two men whispered, and then the black-habited man, gaunt and bent, took me by the hand and led me up a flight of stairs, and suddenly I was standing in a hall that looked like a classroom, only the windows were much higher and the blackboards were much bigger and the benches were much cushier than in my old school, and in this auditorium stood a tall, blonde monk with huge horn-rimmed glasses, and the man who had shown us the way said that this was Father Kornelius Schmid who would give me my entrance examination now, and I should stay nice and calm and not be afraid, and then my father and the monk went out and I was standing by myself in the big room and Father Kornelius Schmid took off his glasses and polished them and said, 'Well, well, li'l 'un, let's see what you've got in that li'l head of yours!' and he poked me in the side and winked and suddenly the whole thing was fun. I stood at the blackboard and did arithmetic and writing and named the names of kings and the dates of battles; the priest asked more and more quickly and I tossed out the knowledge from my memory, it was tremendous fun, and I'd worked myself into a fine frenzy when the blonde priest laughed and said that was enough. In spite of myself I said 'Too bad!' and sighed, and Father Schmid laughed; then my father returned, and he laughed and cried and hugged me, and then we went into an office where two old priests sat, and my father signed a form, and then he counted lots of large bills onto the desk, a wallet full of money, and I was proud because Kalksburg was so incredibly expensive and posh.

Then we drove to Vienna in a taxi; it was the first time I'd ridden in a real, actual car, and I remember how splendidly it stank of gasoline, my head spun, so splendid was the stink, and I sat next to the driver and gazed out at the green, hilly landscape flying past, and I was John Dillinger, the gangster kingpin, escaped from prison yet again and racing to join his gang, with the police in hot pursuit and shooting their pistols like mad, but Dillinger's car was the fastest and its windows were bullet-proof glass. Then the taxi stopped and father paid, and then we were sitting in a fairy-tale hall of gold and crystal that sparkled in all the colours of the rainbow; a waiter in a black tailcoat without a single spot bowed and presented to me on his outstretched arm a silver platter in whose thirty-six hollows lay thirty-six exquisite morsels: sardines and salmon and anchovies and pink curls of meat and little cones of ham, decorated with wafer-thin cucumber slices and garnished with herbs I didn't even know the names of, and a round piece of toast was heaped with little, black fish eggs, and my father said I should try that, it was real Russian caviar. The waiter held the enormous platter serenely on his outstretched arm and said: 'Feel free to help yourself, young man!' I shyly eyed a sardine's back, tenderly draped with a lemon slice, and my father laughed and filled my plate with twelve of the exquisite morsels and emptied twelve of the hollows himself. I took fright at the thought of the price, but my father said that this was the Orderv, the appetizer platter, the famous Orderv Platter of the famous Hotel Sacher where we were dining, and he said it didn't matter if you took one Orderv or the whole platter, it all cost the same, that was what was so posh and first-class about it. I asked why we didn't wrap up the rest and take it with us but father said that wasn't a posh thing to do, we could do that at home in the Rübezahl Tavern, but not here at the Hotel Sacher in Vienna, where counts, princes and ministers dined, the crème de la crème of society, and I glanced round furtively and saw chatting gentlemen in dinner jackets and ladies in silk dresses with flashing rings and bracelets and chains, and one even wore a golden circlet in her piled-up hair, and I pulled myself together so as not to embarrass

Father, and took great pains not to let a morsel slide off my fork. The caviar was oily and salty and I didn't like it one bit but I forced it down because it was the poshest, and my father said it cost a fortune here, that was true, but today he wanted nothing but the very best for me. At that he put his arm round my shoulder and said I'd passed the exam with honours, summa cum laude, with the highest of praise, Father Schmid had said they'd never seen such talent, and then we drank spritzers and the glasses refracted the chandelier light and the soft violins sang their heavenly song. I was happy through and through; I sat intoxicated amid the gold and crystal, and my father said that I couldn't possibly imagine what it meant to become a pupil at Kalksburg, by passing the exam I had stepped through the door to high society, and he listed all the things I could become after graduating from Kalksburg: mayor, envoy, professor, government councillor, member of parliament, state secretary, why, even minister, intimate in the circle of Excellencies, elect among the elect, and I saw gold and crystal and silver tureens and thought that the first thing I'd do when I was famous was print calling cards, because Count H had calling cards, gold-embossed, with a crown and his noble title, and when he visited us he always had the serving girl bring it to my father, and I thought that was the finest and poshest thing in the whole world. The Kalksburgers were a close-knit community, supporting and promoting one another, my father said, and the waiter in the spotless tailcoat served me a slice of beef fried golden brown and wished me a hushed *bon appétit*; and then came a curious change.

Thus far it had all been marvellously quiet; now it turned loud, noise smashed into the chatter of the guests and the singing of the violins, the golden room resounded with footfalls and cries, rhythmic shouts rang out, hoarse hollers. I flinched, my knife and fork clattering on the plate, but round me the guests chatted as though nothing were happening, and the waiter bent down to me with a smile and said that I shouldn't be scared, those were just the good-for-nothing hooligans, demonstrating again. 'Filthy riffraff,' my father said indignantly, and suddenly the rhythm of the voices outside shifted to a roar of rage, and I heard harsh commands and tramping and clattering; I turned round and saw to my horror that they were standing in the middle of the hall, amid the gold and crystal stood three men with twisted faces and stubbly chins and clenched fists swinging menacingly, and I stared into the bronze-framed mirror across from the window and realized that this was the Commune. I had never seen the Commune before, there was no Commune back home, only honest, well-behaved workers who greeted as they were supposed to when they saw my father and stepped aside when he or someone of his rank passed them on the street. The fists rose into the air; I thought of the workers in my father's pharmacy, good old Anton Vojtek and Fritzl Heller and Anna Maschke and the other six: unthinkable for them to clench their fists and yell on the street and rebel like these, the scum, the Commune that ought to be hanged by the heels, as my father always said when he explained the political situation to us over lunch, and I wondered indignantly why they were allowed to do that, clench their fists and yell this way, and why the police, who had finally arrived, didn't throw them all in jail, and then suddenly it was all over, it was quiet again, the conversations hummed softly as always, the woman with the golden circlet in her hair gave a gentleman a smile, and in the bronze-framed mirror across from the window the street lay tranquil in the mild light. My father nudged me: I should eat up, he told me, the steak would get cold. I ate, but it had lost its savour, and as I ate I listened to whether the cries would return, and suddenly I was sorry I hadn't gone out onto the street or at least to the window to stand eye to eye with the Commune, and mechanically I said the words with which my father always ended his lunchtime ruminations: 'Soon the Führer will bring order to the Reich!' I thought my father would agree with me but he stepped on my foot and hissed that I shouldn't talk about Hitler in Kalksburg, people supported Dollfuss here, and besides, my father said, it looked like the Führer wouldn't make it in the Reich, and to my astonished 'Why?' my father said that had to do with the elections and I wouldn't understand until much later. Then we raised our glasses a second and a third time to the bright future and to Kalksburg and to my studies, and I thought defiantly that one day the Führer would prevail after all.

But the day the Führer did prevail has vanished from my memory. I had other worries; I had great trouble submitting to the Spartan discipline of monastic life, to the eternally identical rhythm of grey days that began with Holy Mass and ended with Vespers, divided with implacable precision into hours which, but for breaks, meals and two hours of sports, had to be spent in silence. In silence, lined up two by two, heads bowed as per regulation so that one's gaze rested humbly on the heels of the boy in front, who in turn gazed at the heels of the boy in front of him, we walked down the endless corridors to the chapel and the study hall and the classroom, in silence we knelt on the pew kneelers, in silence we hunched over books and notebooks, and we had to take our punishments in silence: the hazel-rod lashes of the Father Professors and the clouts and rabbit punches of the

Father Prefect who minded us after our lessons, and so the days since my admission had trickled past grey in identical rhythm, and only one shines brighter in my memory: 15 January 1933, my eleventh birthday. On our birthdays and name days we could be sent a ten-pound food package; it was not given to us directly, but the kitchen prefect divided its contents into fourteen daily portions which were set at the fortunate recipient's place at the breakfast table, a very welcome addition to the usual breakfast of malt coffee, a roll and a spoonful of jam. The previous evening at eight o'clock, when the light of the dormitory where we slept in small, curtained wooden cubicles was switched off, I had already thought longingly of the full plate I hoped to find next to my coffee cup the next day, and I'd sent up a quick prayer to Saint Alois, the school's patron saint, for the package to be on time; my first thought at five in the morning, when the Father Prefect's shrill bell woke us, was not, as advised, a devout ejaculation to the Holy Mother of God, but the sinful anticipation of sardines and cookies, and even at Holy Mass I caught myself thinking lustful thoughts of treats. Then, in silence, our heads bowed and our gaze fixed on the heels of the boy in front, we walked down the endless corridor to the study hall where we completed our morning study hour in silence, and then, after the bell, we rose and lined up again two by two, and in silence, with bowed heads, walked back along the endless corridor and down the stairs to the refectory, and defying regulations I raised my eyes, and a full plate indeed stood resplendent at my place. I saw a piece of raisin stollen and a tin of sardines and a chocolate bar and fruit and— opened as always—a letter. Then I stood in silence before these splendours and folded my hands and repeated the blessing spoken by the Father Prefect on duty, and then at last came the signal to sit, and, as no one had raised his head in the corridor and no one had whispered to anyone else, the signal that we could speak. The voices rose in a whir like sparrows swarming from a tree, my neighbours held their plates out for my treasures and I doled out sardines and cookies and apples. Only Friedrich Schiller, the Czech who sat to my left, got nothing; he hadn't given me any of his package either. These breakfast delights lasted two whole weeks, I vividly recall, and then the days were as dreary as ever, and one of those dreary days must have been the day Adolf Hitler seized power in the distant Reich in order to wipe out the Commune, but that I no longer remember. All I know is that we weren't allowed to talk about Hitler at the monastery and that one time there was a big investigation because of a swastika drawn on a blackboard and a group of fifth years was expelled, and I know that I admired those fifth years.

Otherwise I remember little of 1933; but I will never forget one day the following year, a February day with thick sheaths of ice on the trees and crusted snow on the blessing hands of the Virgin's statue in the park. It was the afternoon of Shrove Monday; we had seen the school theatre perform Raimund's *Peasant Turned Millionaire* the day before, listening with feeling to Wurzel's ode to contentment, and now we looked forward to going to the cinema in Rodaun the next day to see the talking picture *The Duke of Reichstadt*. Suddenly—it was third period in the afternoon and we were having our sports break—the lights went out and the gymnasium was plunged into gloom. I was annoyed, because I was playing table tennis and missed an easy shot, but then, along with the others, I gloated over this favourable sign; the three-hour afternoon-study period began in fifteen minutes, but with no light it would likely be cancelled. I remember that we betted on whether the light would return by the beginning of the study period; I bet against and my friend, the slender, delicate Count Staffperg, bet for; I know that I won: the lights stayed out in the murky room, and then someone in the corridor called the Father Prefect. The Father Prefect, a short man with a pinched face, came down from his pulpit-like lectern and went outside. In a little while he returned with a burning candle in his hand and said that we should sit down and he would read to us from a funny book. Nothing like that had ever happened before, and as he spoke, or so it seemed to me, his otherwise so sibilantly sharp voice trembled, and suddenly I and the others turned restive. Had something happened? Why weren't the lights back on? Last winter the lights had gone out once too, but the problem had been fixed in a few minutes, and now we'd gone over an hour without light! The Father Prefect read the story of Bill of the Black Hand; though I was hardly listening, I noticed him stumble several times. Then suddenly I heard strange explosive sounds, like a burst of dry coughing, and little Liechtenberg cried out: 'They're shooting!' and we jumped up, and suddenly everyone was screaming, and then the door flew open and the Father Prefect from the class next door came running in to ask if we'd heard it too, and then came several overlapping bursts of coughing, and suddenly we were all milling in the corridor. Unbelievably, inconceivably, we ran screaming down the corridor where not a word was supposed to fall, and we heard that the Reds had occupied the power plant and there was shooting in Liesing and Hitzing and Mödling and then we heard that Vienna was burning, the Reds had set Vienna on fire and now they were marching on to Kalksburg! Then we all knelt in the chapel before the image of the Immaculate Virgin Mary, and the Father General Prefect knelt before the altar and read the prayer to the holy Archangel Michael, the warrior with the flaming sword: 'O Glorious Prince of the heavenly host,' we heard, 'St Michael the Archangel, defend us in the battle and in the terrible warfare that we are waging against the evil spirits. Come to the aid of man, whom Almighty God created immortal, made in His own image and likeness, fight this day the battle of the Lord, together with the holy angels, as already thou hast fought the leader of the proud angels, Lucifer, and his apostate host, for whom there was no place any longer in Heaven!' He chanted the sacred words, nearly singing the word heaven, and the drawn-out syllables echoed in the vast room that swallowed the hanging lamps' red light. All round in the altar niches the statues of the saints raised their waxen hands, and their golden robes cascaded down. 'Arise then, O invincible Prince, bring help against the attacks of the lost spirits to the people of God,' chanted the Father General Prefect, and in the distance a machine gun went rat-a-tat-tat. Then the Father General Prefect recited the Litany of the Immaculate Conception, and on our knees, in extremis, we cried out to heaven 'Pray for us':

'Queen of all saints and angels,

pray for us;

Terror and defeater of evil spirits,

pray for us!'

and in the oil lamp's fading glow I saw the gentle
features of the saint I had so often gazed at during
Mass: the high, white brow and the brown hair and
the soft mouth with the narrow, barely curved lips,
and I saw the red glow wash over her face and
begged: Pray, oh pray for us! and outside, closer,
the machine gun hammered. Then we crowded
into the dormitory, where candles stood on the
partitions between the cubicles, the Father Prefect
urged us to address a devout ejaculation to the Virgin Mary or the Holy Archangel Michael, and the
candles were snuffed; I crawled under the covers
and thought with a shudder of all the things I knew
about the Commune: they were criminals and
didn't want to work and they wanted to take everything away from the honest people because they
were too lazy and they pillaged and murdered and
stole whatever they could get their hands on and
gave rhythmic shouts and clenched their fists and
they'd stood in the middle of the splendid gold-
and-crystal hall and clenched their fists and gave
rhythmic shouts and now they'd set Vienna on fire
and were marching on to Kalksburg, and I decided
to die as a martyr for the Virgin. No, I wouldn't
deny the Holy Madonna, I'd stride forth to face
the mob, my Queen's image in my heart and the

Saviour's cross in my hands, and outside, closer, the machine gun hammered.

Then I fell asleep, and when I woke up again the dark morning droned and reverberated, the windows rattled; jumping out of bed, I heard the voice of the Father Prefect saying that the Holy Mother of God had heard our prayers, the Reds had been forced to retreat, Mödling had already been liberated and the heroic fighters of the Home Guard were shelling the Red districts to smithereens. The morning reverberated, the windows rattled; I washed and dressed and then waited in my cubicle for the bell that would summon us to line up in silence, two by two, and march to the chapel. I was feverish with impatience; a calendar lay on the shelf above my bed but I didn't want to read now. Feverish with impatience, I even thought of making my bed but then I let it be; it had been impressed upon us that that was the servants' work. I bit my tongue, burning to go over to Hans Staffperg in the cubicle next door and ask if he wanted to become a martyr with me but I couldn't leave my cubicle before the signal, and above all I couldn't speak; breakfast, if all went well, was the first time we could speak each day, and the three hours until then seemed infinitely long. The morning reverberated, the candles on the cubicles flickered, the handbell shrilled, we

parted the curtains and stepped out from our
cubicles and lined up two by two with bowed
heads as per regulation, and then, slowly, each gazing at the heels of the boy in front, we walked
down the endless corridor to the chapel to say our
morning prayers, and I saw the heels of the boy in
front of me, these eternal heels and the endless corridor we walked down dozens of times a day this
way, and I realized with horror that I would have
to walk this way for seven more years, head bowed,
and suddenly my chest grew tight and I looked up
and the Father Prefect's fist struck my neck. It was
a weak blow and a fleeting pain; the Father Prefect
hadn't struck with all his strength; I bowed my
head again and saw the endless corridor and suddenly a wild red wave seemed to rush through my
blood. My temples throbbed; I dug my nails into
the balls of my hands, and suddenly I knew something I'd known for a long time, from the first day
I'd seen them: Yes, I thought, they should come,
let the Reds come, let them come with axes and
knives and firebrands and knock down all of this,
all of it, all of it, the monastery, the walls, the
corridors, the chapel, the statues, the altars, all of
it, all of it, and let them slaughter everyone, the
Fathers, the servants, the pupils, all of them, slice
up the pictures, Alois and Mary and Michael, all of
it, and let them ram their knives into the paunches
under the habits and slit the Papist throats, yes, let

them, and let them set fires, big, red, devouring
fires, destroying all of this, and if they cut my
throat too, what of it, as long as they don't leave a
single stone standing! I knew what I was thinking
was a deadly sin, perhaps even the unforgivable sin
against the Holy Spirit, but even that didn't matter,
so I'd go to Hell, what did I care! During Mass I
went cold and shivers wracked me and then the
fever came on and the Father Prefect took me to
the infirmary and I lay in bed delirious and dreamt
of fires and Madonnas and goat-legged devils with
sweat dripping from their bellies, and in the middle of the night I woke up soaking wet and thought
I was going to die. The next morning I wrote a note
to Father Kornelius, now my confessor, and asked
him to hear my confession, and then I confessed
my sinful thoughts of rebellion to him in a cell
hung with oilcloth, and Father Kornelius ques-
tioned me for a long time and asked whether I had
discussed this with other pupils and whether anyone else believed the Commune should come, and
I shook my head and said that I alone bore the
blame. Then, as penance, Father Kornelius commanded me to pray to Saint Alois for the blessing
of humility which I lacked, and then he made the
sign of the cross over me and absolved me. Once
recovered, I did as he had ordered and tried for two
years to achieve the blessing of humility; then one
evening I climbed over the wall of the park and

fled home and resolved never to return to the monastery, however my father might rage and yell. But my father didn't rage, in fact, he didn't even scold me; he seized me tight and admitted that he sometimes worried about my future and would have taken me out of the boarding school at the end of the year anyway, for world history, he said, and his eyes shone, had begun to march with iron strides, and it was quite clear that the future belonged not to the reactionary clergy, but to Adolf Hitler's Germany, to which the Sudeten region would also belong someday. I fell into his arms, speechless with joy, and the next day I joined the German Gymnastics Society, the youth organization of the Sudeten Fascists; my former schoolmates congratulated me on not having to return to the monastery, and donning the grey uniform of the Gymnastics Society I breathed a sigh of relief, liberated by the knowledge that the world was now set right for good!

The gymnasium in Reichenberg—after leaving Kalksburg I was now attending secondary school in what was then the capital of Sudeten Fascism, about twenty miles from my home town—lives on in my memory as an olive-black hulk that flanked a steeply climbing lane. Its defence must have taken place around 15 September 1938, at a time when we heard hair-raising reports thrice a day on German radio about the bloody terror wreaked by the Czech-Jewish-Marxist cutthroats upon the peaceful Sudeten German population, along with the Führer's assurances that a major power like the German Reich was no longer willing to stand by and watch as defenceless German brothers and sisters beyond its borders suffered at the hands of a nation of *Untermenschen*, and that the Sudeten German question must be solved, one way or the other. In Reichenberg, not a German had been so much as injured yet, and I hadn't heard anything of the kind from my hometown either, in fact the Czech border post had been attacked and set on fire, but in all the other Sudeten German towns, we heard, there had already been the most appalling atrocities against Germans and the fiercest battles had raged, and when barbed-wire barricades appeared on the Reichenberg market-place one morning and armed police patrolled and my team captain Karli yelled to me breathlessly that the Czechs were going to attack the Reichen-berg gymnasium, I knew that now it was Reichen-berg's turn and my hour of truth had come.

I was ready. Just a month before, I had gazed at the face of the Führer himself and sworn him eternal fealty. Along with thousands of my com-rades from the Gymnastics Society I had taken part in the 1938 Greater German Gymnastics and Sports Festival in Breslau; eight abreast we'd marched into the stadium chanting 'We want to go home to the Reich', the new slogan that epitomized all we were and yearned for, and in the stands all round the people cheered us and clapped and stamped and waved hands and kerchiefs and flags and sang songs and everything was like a dream, a billowing, bellowing, jubilant dream, but then this was Germany, realm of German joy and German freedom! We marched down the stadium track, and I glanced round furtively for the Führer, who had to be standing somewhere in the jubilant crowd, but I saw nothing but the stadium track and above it the bellowing stands, where I couldn't make out the faces; to the right and left of the track were walls of SS men and we'd marched down the whole length of the track and I was sad that I'd missed the Führer, when suddenly we entered a curve, meeting a column from the opposite direction, a march blared out and drowned our chorus, and there in the stands stood the Führer, so close before us in the blazing floodlights, so close and tall and alone, a god of history, and he raised his hand over us and his eyes swept our ranks and I thought my heart would stop when the Führer looked at me, and suddenly I knew my life was consecrated to the Führer forevermore.

Then we'd driven back across the border in the car my father had bought the year before; the Czech customs official searched our suitcases, and there was a long dispute between him and my father because the customs official had found ten packs of cigarettes among the underwear in the suitcase and said we had to pay customs on them, and my father shouted that it was an outrage that a German couldn't even smoke German cigarettes in this country without the Prague Jews earning off them, and then the customs official simply took away the cigarettes and tore open the packs and tossed them into a ditch where a pile of torn-open German cigarette packs already lay, and I trembled with rage at having to stand defenceless in the face of this robbery and clenched my fists and thought that soon the hour of freedom must strike. Three weeks later, German radio reported that the Führer had called a million reservists to arms, and soon after that I had a fight with my father, because he wanted to send my mother, sister and me to business contacts in Vienna during this critical phase. I vehemently refused to leave; historic days were approaching, I said, and I wanted to witness them and fight if need be; finally my father gave in, and I returned to Reichenberg. And one September morning, in the dawn of a grey, foggy day, my friend Karli knocked on the window of my ground-floor student quarters at Frau Waclawek's on Gablonzer Strasse and yelled to me breathlessly that I had to come to the gymnasium quickly, it was an orange alert, today the Czechs would attack the gymnasium! Then he'd run on to tell the others and I'd set out for the gymnasium, walking down Gablonzer Strasse. It was a cold morning, and now, I thought, the hour of truth had come.

I was excited: I'd never been in a battle like this; the occasional school scuffles didn't count, the scouting games and the stupid provocations of the police in which I and all the others indulged; now it would turn serious, a real battle with real weapons, and I felt my heart beating, and wondered suddenly how it feels when a knife slips between the ribs. My steps faltered; I didn't think about the knife, I saw it, gleaming, and as I passed Ferdl, a sausage vendor who stood not far from the gymnasium, I even thought of stealing off down an alley, but then I scolded myself and walked quickly into the building.

Two sentries at the portal, guards in the corridor; password: Germany; the sentries stepped aside, the door slammed shut behind me. Now there was no turning back, and here, among my comrades, my fear suddenly turned to the lust to see battle soon. It was dark in the gymnasium hall: the windows had been barricaded from floor to gable with sandbags and mats, and only a skylight in the flat roof admitted a ray of sun into the enormous room. I looked round for a leader I could report to, and saw there was no lack of leaders; they wore armbands with the victory rune and hurried busily to and fro, sending scouts up to the flat roof, assembling groups, platoons and companies and distributing clubs and iron dumbbells and other gymnastics equipment as weapons. I was given a club of heavy brown oak, a long club with a handy knob and a massive shaft: I see it before me now, and I remember giving it a casual swing to try it out. 'They have revolvers too!' my neighbour whispered, pointing his chin at the leaders. 'Attention!'

yelled a burly man. Our heels clicked together. It's serious, now it's serious, I thought, standing at attention and picturing how the foe would soon come charging through the door, the fearsome foe, the Bolshevik mob: they'd come charging through the door, and the alarm would sound and the battle would begin, a real battle, no war game now, a real battle for Germany, and I weighed the club in my hand, standing shoulder to shoulder with my comrades. The burly man spoke of our fealty to the Führer and the Germans' right to self-determination and then he cried: 'Victory or death!' and we repeated it in chorus. Then we were dismissed; the company I belonged to, all young lads my age, was instructed to form a reserve in the equipment room and wait for orders there. We went to the equipment room and sat down, our weapons at the ready; for a time there was an awkward silence, and then one guy said that the Reds should come if they liked, we'd damn well show them, and then we drowned one another out yelling that we'd damn well show the Reds when they arrived, and one guy yelled shrilly that they wouldn't even dare to come, those Reds, and we yelled again, and then one guy began telling a joke, and we told one another all the old gags and dirty jokes we knew, and we laughed at them too, and this laughter, like the yelling before, sounded much too loud. Then all the jokes had been told, and we sat silently again

and waited for the foe, but the foe didn't come—
we sat and waited; the foe didn't come; conversations crumbled, laughter turned to grumbling. Time
stood still; the foe kept us waiting and waiting. In its
place came something dreadful: boredom.

Just when this boredom came, I no longer
know but I believe little time passed from the
moment I entered the gymnasium to boredom's
onset. It must have been early in the day still when
boredom came to the gloomy, barely lit equipment
room, and it came as something tangible, a stale,
slow-roiling effluvium that crept about us, settling
sluggishly—no mental product but a purely physical one given off by a huddle of humanity like
sweat or used-up air. We waited, and this waiting
bred boredom—our mission was to wait, and so
we waited and did nothing else, and it would have
been inconceivable to me to take a book out of my
pocket and read or do a crossword puzzle or start
a conversation with a friend on some intellectual
topic or doze, much less sleep: all these things
would have seemed subversive to me somehow,
frivolous and unheroic, incommensurate with the
pathos of our mission, and the others must have
felt as I did, for we all sat this way and waited, and
boredom surged sluggishly about us. My eye-
lids drooped and my head sagged forward; for a
moment I nodded off, then roused myself again,
ashamed, and here and there a head fell forward

and jerked up again, and we sat this way and listened in growing desperation for the alarm to be given at last, the liberating alarm that would launch us into battle, but the alarm wasn't given. We stared at one another bleary-eyed. The room was dark and the air was stuffy. The foe didn't come. What came, slowly but with growing force, was hunger.

As we usually bought hot sausages and pretzels from the school caretaker at recess, few had sandwiches along, and those who did had soon eaten them. As for the rest of us, our stomachs growled. Finally the company leader set out to inform headquarters of the provisioning problem. Soon he returned with instructions for the company to assemble a volunteer raiding party to break through to Ferdl the Sausage Man at the end of the street, purchase sausages with horseradish, rolls and beer and transport the spoils back to the gymnasium. The other companies, the company leader said, striding up and down, would also send out raiding parties, but the troop movement must happen quickly so as not to weaken the gymnasium's defences for long; it was quite possible, said the company leader, that if the foe detected the temporary weakness, he would exploit it to attack the gymnasium; so as not to arouse suspicion, the individual raiding parties should keep their distance and give no signs of knowing one another. We asked whether weapons should be carried, and the company leader responded in the negative: no weapons should be carried, he said, but to guard against sudden attacks by the Reds two protective flanks would be formed, though for purposes of camouflage they should carry no weapons either. 'Who volunteers?' asked the company leader, and I leapt up and volunteered eagerly; many others leapt up and volunteered, but I was lucky; I was standing near the company leader and got assigned to the raiding party's right protective flank. The raiding party and the entire operation was headed by my friend Karli. We gathered in the gymnasium hall, and Karli gave us our final instructions: to deceive the foe, we wouldn't go straight to Ferdl the Sausage Man; instead, we'd go up the street in the opposite direction, then turn onto a side alley, go back down the parallel street, and finally reach Ferdl the Sausage Man's stand via a shopping arcade, making our purchases one by one at discreet intervals and returning to the gymnasium by the same route. 'Is everything clear?' asked Karli. We nodded. We walked across the hall; sentries at the door, guards in the corridor, sentries at the portal, clubs and iron mallets, password: Germany. The door opened a crack. We slipped out. The noon light made us squint. In front of us, in the noon light, lay the town we'd known for years. We squinted. We'd never seen the town this way before.

We had never seen the town this way before, though it looked the same as ever: the arcades with the vegetable stands, at noon no longer thronged by the housewives with their bags and baskets; children hauled jugs of beer from the pub; cats sunned themselves in the gutter; the beggar on the street corner sung his litany; the men in the cafe clustered round billiard and tarock games; a daytime whore touched up her lips; news dealers hawked their wares; the windows of the Bat'a shop glittered in the sun and behind them paced the elegant salesman, blond as a brush, while advertisements for Shell Oil and Stollwerck chocolates screamed from the facade. The town lay in the mild noon light, the fog had fled, the town looked the same as ever, the familiar picture barely altered by the barricade on the market-place, and yet it was no longer the town we knew: it was enemy territory, grey, embrasures in the houses and snipers behind them, the foe lurking out there somewhere, the arcades eerie, no-man's-land! We flitted up the street, protective flanks and raiding party, and everything seemed ghostly, unreal; we were at war, we were in action, I was a schoolboy no longer, I was the second man in the right protective flank of the reserve company's provisioning party, and if I'd had a revolver, I'd have had the right to gun down any foe, any Red, any Bolshevik like the young man over there hawking a special edition of *Die Rote Fahne*; we were in battle, and we flitted like ghosts through the streets; it was a puerile game, and the ghastly thing was that this puerile game could launch forth a murder at any moment like a live bullet from a stage pistol. It was a puerile game we were playing, childish antics, and yet murderous, and the awful thing was that we felt neither the puerility nor the murderousness. We were in action, under orders, advancing through enemy territory, and so, the five-man shopping commando in the middle and the three-man protective flanks to the left and right, we casually strolled up the street, turned off without incident, made our way back down the parallel street through the tide of workers, Germans and Czechs coming from the morning shift, cut through the arcade, side by side, and at discreet intervals each bought twenty pairs of sausages with rolls and beer. 'Do you have practice today? You're the third bunch already to come for sausages,' said Ferdl the Sausage Man, beaming. We didn't bat an eye. 'The other guys who were here, they aren't with us,' said Karli, head of the raiding party, thinking quickly. Down the street came the fourth party. 'Got you!' said Ferdl the Sausage Man, winking. The fourth raiding party had reached the stand. We didn't know one another. 'Twenty pairs of sausages with rolls and beer,' said the head of the fourth raiding party.

Ferdl the Sausage Man grinned. Our raiding party took the sausages, rolls and beer, strode poker-faced towards the arcade, cut through, went up the parallel street, now with the tide of workers, turned off, strode down the main street, past the market stands and the cafe with the tarock players and the daytime whores and the ad for Shell Oil, and Karli, head of the raiding party, pounded his fist on the portal, three short knocks and one long; the door opened a crack; double sentries, password: Germany! We flitted inside, guards in the corridor, sentries at the door, cudgels and clubs; the hall; darkness; we were back. The raiding party dropped off the sausages in the equipment room, and Karli reported the execution of the order to the company leader. 'Mission accomplished without incident!' Karli finished. 'Fall in for chow!' the company leader ordered. We munched away. And then boredom returned.

Impossible to describe this afternoon: the mired march of the hours, each minute seeming an eternity, the turbid bubbles of obscenity that swelled in the brain and sluggishly burst, the whistling snores of the spirit, the sour, flat beer fumes, the tedium of the callisthenics which we performed in groups from time to time and which only stirred up the effluvium of boredom. Time flowed like tallow congealing, its taste stale in our throats. No foe; the guards patrolled in the corridor outside, we heard their clacking steps and let grunts slip into the sleepy hours and heard the clacking of steps in the corridor, when suddenly a shout rolled down from the roof like thunder: the roof scouts shouted to the messenger and the messenger shouted to the corridor guards, and we heard the corridor guards shout 'Alarm!' and grabbed our weapons and bolted into the hall.

The burly man stood in the hall and shouted 'Alarm!' and we ran to and fro and lined up in rank and file, and we were scarcely lined up before it happened: past the door sentries and accompanied by the rows of the corridor guards, a Czech police lieutenant strode into the hall, a wiry little man followed by two older police officers, and we clenched our fists round our weapons and trembled with lust for battle, and the burly man stepped forward and walked towards the Czech lieutenant, weighing the iron dumbbells in his hands, and the Czech lieutenant touched his hand to his kepi and said: 'Good efening, chentlemen' and the burly man raised the dumbbells in front of his chest.

I trembled.

'And vat, pray tell, are you chentlemen doing?' asked the lieutenant. 'We're doing gymnastics,' the burly man said hoarsely. I felt the blood pounding in my temples; now the order would come to pounce upon the foe! 'Chymnastics, it is healthy,' said the lieutenant, raising his left hand and turning back his cuff with the right; 'it is very healthy,' he repeated and pushed back his cuff and said a third time, smiling, that gymnastics was very healthy, and added, looking at his watch, that he hadn't wanted to disturb us gentlemen and would be on his way again; he only wanted to point out, and he held up his watch to the burly man's eyes, that it was already a quarter after seven, and eight was curfew, wasn't it, because of the state of emergency being declared, and he said some of the gentlemen might have a long way home and he'd hate for them to be rushed, and he pushed his cuff back over his watch, touched his hand to his kepi and turned round, saying as he turned: 'I vish the chentlemen an enchoyable efening' and strolled out the door, the two policemen following him at a leisurely pace. We stared at one another—what had just happened couldn't have been real, it had to have been a trick of the senses, a hallucination, a phantasm; we stared at one another, dumbfounded, and then we stared at our leader, and what happened after that, I don't quite remember, all I know is that everything happened very quickly and that the burly man said something like 'Mission accomplished' and 'Our day will come' and 'The plot has been foiled', and I know I tossed away the club and set out briskly; I had a long way home.

The next morning we heard a report on German radio about the latest horrific atrocity by the Czech-Jewish-Marxist cutthroats: a horde of brutish police troops, we heard, had stormed the Reichenberg gymnasium, falling upon harmless schoolboys at their gymnastics exercises and flouting all principles of ethnic self-determination by going on a most inhuman rampage among the boys, who defended themselves heroically; there were deaths and many injuries, the radio reported, blood had spilt in rivers on the gymnasium floor; the children's desperate cries had resounded to the heavens, mingled with the howls and shrieks of the Red mob and the clear commanding voices of the heroic defenders, and a major power like the German Reich could no longer bear to stand by and watch as these atrocities were inflicted upon its brothers and sisters outside the borders. I listened to this report, which ended with a rendition of the Egerland March, with Karli in my room at Frau Waclawek's on Gablonzer Strasse; we listened to this report knowing every word for a lie and yet we listened with eyes aglow and it never crossed our mind that it was all just lies. 'Man, that little Goebbels sure knows his propaganda,' said Karli, head of my raiding party, and punched me in the ribs, 'no one's ever done propaganda like that

before, that's just grand!' and Karli said that no
other country but the Reich could pull off propaganda that grand, and I nodded. He was right.

A few days later, in Munich, the heads of state of
England, France, Italy and Germany agreed to
carve up Czechoslovakia.

First it was a rumour that came down the mountains, leaping like the flicker of lightning into the taprooms' smoky gloom: the region where our town was situated wouldn't be ceded to the Reich at all, this awful rumour claimed; instead, since the villages all round were inhabited entirely by Czechs, it would remain part of the Czech rump state. The rumour galvanized us. 'If those French and English are too stupid to bring us home to the Reich, then we'll just have to do it ourselves!' my father shouted when the rumour reached the Rübezahl Tavern, and banged his fist on the table so hard that the beer glasses clashed. We were sitting in the Rübezahl Tavern; these days everyone sat in his favourite pub to discuss the political situation, and so we sat discussing the political situation in the Rübezahl Tavern near the marketplace. Things looked bleak: the bulk of the Sudeten region had already been annexed in accordance with the Munich Agreement; only our town and the surrounding villages in the Giant Mountains hadn't been annexed yet, and now came the rumour that we wouldn't be annexed at all. 'If those French and English are that stupid, then we'll just liberate ourselves!' my father shouted and banged his fist on the table, and everyone sitting drinking beer in the Rübezahl Tavern yelled 'Bravo!' and 'Get out the guns!' and 'Freedom!' and we drank beer and kummel and sang in chorus: 'Giant Mountains, German mountains' but then Dohnt, who had his farm up on the mountain ridge, came bursting into the taproom and shouted that we should come quick, the Czechs were pulling out. After all that! We rushed out. The Czech soldiers came down from the mountains.

Down from the mountains, from their supposedly impregnable border fortifications, the Czech soldiers filed, a narrow olive-yellow ribbon unrolling down the pastures' green slope into the valley, a weary column now filing down the road through town. They walked in silence, with dragging steps and hanging heads, their faces dark and filled with shame; they were exhausted and bedraggled, they'd stood guard at their posts, they'd been eager to fight, prepared to die, and now they had been ordered to abandon their fortifications and trenches and bunkers and ramparts without firing a shot, and they came down from the mountains in their olive-yellow uniforms, heads hanging, an army betrayed. They marched without a word;

some clenched their fists, some wept. Their shoes were covered in dust. The soldiers were silent, a long, mute procession and we stood on the curb outside the pub watching them, silent too, a jeering silence. 'Get lost!' a guest yelled from the pub window. The soldiers walked wearily, out of step. One stumbled. One pressed his fists to his temples. The rifles bounced on their backs. One's rifle sling was torn; he carried his rifle on a rope. We stared at him, everyone stared at him; we didn't know why his rifle sling was torn, we merely noted scornfully that he had a rope for a rifle sling. The soldier with his rifle on a rope hung his head; he was a hulking lad, and he hung his head, and his cheeks burnt. Beyond the marketplace they vanished from our sight; then a few stragglers appeared; finally two soldiers came propping up a third who hobbled on one leg; they trudged slowly down the road, and then they vanished from our sight as well. Were we free now? We didn't know. A wind surged; it smelt of pears and hay. I breathed deeply and looked up at the mountains: the twin brown domes of the summits rose into the sky like the bosom of a goddess bedded on the pastures. The sun was at its zenith; the summits gleamed as though clad in copper mail. The wind had died down, it was utterly still, when uphill from the road we heard a hammering and crashing, and the hammering and crashing came down the road and grew louder and louder and suddenly we too began to swarm the marketplace like hornets and now we too were storming the school and the town hall and the public buildings and shops and workshops and offices and taverns and street signs. Waking from our stupor, we realized all at once: we were free now, the Czechs were gone, everything was German now, now we determined things ourselves, self-determination had come at last, and now for those bilingual plaques and company names and street signs: ŠKOLA crashed down from the school and RADNICE from the town hall and HOSTINEC from the tavern; we ran home, to the orange-red plastered building with the big glass window displaying mortars and medicines in the middle of the ground floor with APOTHEKE in big brass-yellow block letters on the left and LEKÁRNA on the right. I ran for the ladder, the apprentice ran for hammer and pliers, and then, hammered free, the L and the E and the K and the A with its accent and the R and the N and the A went flying to the ground, Czech brass, enemy metal, that was a thing of the past now, now everything would be different, now we determined things; now everything was German, and if a Czech got sick, he'd just have to speak German and know that a pharmacy was called *Apotheke* and not *Lekárna*, and we didn't want any Czechs here anyway, this here was German territory, let them pack off to their brothers in Prague or, better yet, straight to Moscow, they were all Bolsheviks, the lot of them, and if they wouldn't go willingly, we'd help them on their way! The letters flew to the ground now; letters flew to the ground now everywhere; I stood on the ladder hammering off the letters, leaving huge holes in the plaster, but that didn't matter now, quick, quick, down with the letters, the plaster crumbled, a piece of brass struck the window, the tall, wide, costly, frosted window, no other shop in town had a window so tall and wide and costly, and the tall, wide, costly, frosted-glass pane shattered, but that didn't matter now either, as long as the building was free from Czech letters! The letters went flying to the ground, letters flew to the ground everywhere, at last, at last the tavern was simply called *Gasthaus* and not *Gasthaus/Hostinec*, and the restaurant wasn't *Restaurant/Restaurace*, it was only German now, only *Restaurant*, that was freedom, only *Restaurants* and no *Restauraces*, now *we'd* determine that! I knocked off the letter N and tossed it to the ground, all round now letters were flying to the ground, and the wooden signs and the national coat of arms with the lion and the colours white, red and blue; there was a hammering and clashing and clanging and crunching and cracking and splintering and rumbling, it was the blaring of the new time about to dawn, and suddenly, amid this hammering and clanging and crashing and rumbling and blaring, the news resounded like a peal of bells: They're coming!

Dust whirled on the road, marching songs roared, marching feet rang, rise up, you red red eagle: they were coming, they were coming, the Wehrmacht was here! Man, those were soldiers, a band out in front with a drum major and kettledrums and trumpets all aglitter, and what soldiers, man oh man, nothing like those Czechs just now! How they marched, how they sang, what a clangour and a clatter, in lockstep, man, sharp as pins, that was a sight for sore eyes! The Czech soldiers hadn't sung, they'd stumbled down the street with hanging heads, a sad procession, without boots even, just puttees, pathetic, puttees instead of boots, and a rifle on a bit of rope, they'd all had their rifles on bits of rope, a run-down rabble, but that here, now *that* was a sight for sore eyes! Those were soldiers, German soldiers, Germanic blood, you saw the difference at once, they were wearing boots, tall black boots, and their rifles were shouldered, all the same height, not one an inch higher, these were men, Lord Almighty, men like trees, men like bears, and then came a troop of sappers, wiry little devils, small, but oh, they'd aced it, and the Czechs had hulks of men and they'd run off down the mountains without firing a shot—from these sharp little guys, from these strapping lads, these devils, our liberators; the kettledrums banged and the trumpets brayed, rise up, you red red eagle, and we shouted *Heil* and *Heil* again and the tears sprang to our eyes and the soldiers came down the street, and suddenly we all ran towards our liberators, there was no holding us back now, and suddenly the marching order was swept away and we were in one another's arms stammering and weeping and laughing and shouting *Heil* and Welcome and hugging one another, and the children went and got flowers, the last flowers from the gardens, asters and late dahlias, flowers came raining down from all the windows, and with the flowers the flags came fluttering out of the windows, the swastika flags sewn in secret, and the flags waved in the wind and billowed and we were a swirling swarm trampling the Czech letters and coats of arms and flags and hugging our liberators, and all I remember is that I was in heaven, laughing and shouting. Then the columns tried to regroup and march on but we blocked the way; we brought wine and fruit and sandwiches and cake and milk, and the soldiers didn't know where to hold the sandwiches and where to hold their rifles, and slowly, singing, cheering, stammering, the procession poured down the street to the marketplace, liberators and liberated, and the procession kept stalling in the floods of exultation, and at one point it came to a stop in front of the furrier's house, and suddenly through the shouts of *Heil* and the cheering and exulting and weeping came laughter, first a splutter, then a roar of laughter, and the soldiers stood there looking at the furrier's sign and laughed and poked one another in the ribs and held their sides with laughter, and we stared at the sign that had provoked such inordinate laughter, and we laughed along with them without even knowing why, until one of the soldiers, already gasping with laughter, wheezed out: 'Gawd, I nearly split a gut— the guy's really called Kurbel-Arse!'

Of course, we saw it too now, and now we held our sides with laughter—the guy, the furrier, was really called Kurbel-Arse. We'd seen his sign thousands of times without a chuckle—the Czech ending *-ař*, pronounced *arzh*, corresponds to the German suffix *-er*: a baker is *pekař*, a customs officer is *centař*, a grocer is *kramař* and so the furrier was called *Kurbelař*, and he wrote it the German way, hence *Kurbelarsch*, a perfectly ordinary name, and we must have heard it and read it a thousand times and never found it funny, but these soldiers had spotted it—*Kurbelarsch*, Kurbel-Arse, man, we had to be blind: Kurbel-Arse, and we held our sides with laughter and Karli made an obscene gesture and Anton Kurbelarsch the furrier averred with tears of shame and rage that he couldn't help his name, he wasn't a Czech, he was a German, a good German, and as long as anyone could remember there'd never been any Czechs in the family, and first thing tomorrow, no, today if he could, he'd get his name changed to Kurbelar or better yet Kurbler, yes, Kurbler or Kürbler or Körbler, that'd be a German name, and the soldiers gave the furrier a cheerful clap on the shoulder and said he should do just that, because now he was liberated, and Kurbelarsch the furrier said he still couldn't quite believe that he was really liberated and the Czechs wouldn't come back again, and I still couldn't quite believe it either, and the soldiers laughed and said we could bet our lives on it, we were free for good now and the Czechs would never come back, and then the marching column regrouped and the Turkish crescent jingled and the kettledrums boomed and the trumpets brayed, and the soldiers marched onto the marketplace in perfect step, and their rifles all pointed in one direction, and they marched to the marketplace and from there to their quarters. We were assigned a sergeant major; I ceded him my room and bedded down in the attic, and Father fetched the long-hoarded bottle of vintage Steinwein from the cellar; twenty years it had lain there, dust and cobwebs had swathed it, but today was the day at last—at long last freedom had come!

Freedom had come, and I see her as I write, striding down the mountains with the wind in her hair: she had red boots and bare thighs and a wild face whose mouth smelt of kummel and corn schnapps. She came to the taverns and taprooms and there she set up camp; she reigned for a week, and in this week the whole town was one great tavern and one great brothel. We celebrated our freedom with a gigantic binge; there was no school, those who didn't have to go to the factory or the office sat in the pub, and even the soldiers rarely seemed to be on duty. The taprooms were open day and night, the curfew was lifted, my father slipped me a hundred-crown bill and said we must celebrate these historic days, coming generations might not see such days for millennia, and so we celebrated, and celebrating meant: Storm the pubs and broach the kegs! We stopped in the Rübezahl Tavern and the Goldener Stern and the Blauer Ochse and the Hotel Hähnel and the Bergschlösschen and the Hüttenbachbaude and Café Neumann, and there were soldiers sitting everywhere, infantry, artillery, tank drivers, signal-men and sappers, sitting everywhere and drinking, and damn, could they drink, a bottle and another bottle and another schnapps and another pint and another litre and another litre and of course it was our treat, they were our liberators, after all, and we linked arms and swayed back and forth in rows, through the pubs and through the streets; we stopped in every pub, and the merchants who didn't have a bar simply cleared their parlours and set up crates of beer and bottles of schnapps and chairs and tables, and we stopped there too, and all of us had money in our pockets, be it our very last nest egg. We stopped everywhere, there was swilling everywhere and singing everywhere, and we linked arms with our liberators and swayed and swilled and sang the latest song our liberators had brought: 'On the Heath There Grows a Flower Wee' we sang and boom, boom, boom, thrice our fists struck the table till the glasses clashed, and if they broke, no problem, the barkeeper was there with new ones and didn't grumble like he usually did when something got broken, because these were great times for him. These were great times for all the barkeepers and merchants, money from all pockets swelled their tills, they could have used a dozen hands to rake it in, and they hauled the crates of schnapps up from the cellars, whole years' supplies, entire crates behind the bar where otherwise two or three half-empty bottles stood, and everyone spent the last of his money, because glorious times were at hand—no more debts, no cares, no Jews, no times of need—and so we tossed our money on the table: another round for the house! and the barkeeper served up the round for the house and sweat beaded his greasy cheeks and we tossed back the round and drummed on the tables and sang the song about the heath, and then 'She called her son Sylvester for the night of sylvan pleasure', and 'My girl must have black-brown hair, just as black as mine', and then the girls came. The girls came, each one wanted a soldier now, a soldier of her own, and from the villages where no soldiers were billeted they came to our town where the soldiers had their quarters, and each one got a soldier, or two or three or four of them, and the prudes came too, and lo and behold, even they let the soldiers put their hands up their skirts, and the soldiers put their hands up their skirts and hiked up their skirts and gave the bare thighs a slap and undid the blouses and reached in and the girls squealed and the women moaned and the music played, music everywhere, even just a harmonica, and the girls snuggled up to their soldiers, and there was dancing everywhere, everyone danced, in all the taprooms and pubs and the cleared-out parlours there was dancing, and then the couples vanished out into the night, out into the day, there was neither night nor day and couples everywhere, kisses everywhere, panting everywhere, and the music played, day and night the music played and day and night the pubs were open, and it had to go on like this forever, forever and ever, forever and ever, and no one knew if it was day or night or if they were sober or drunk, everyone was babbling,

babbling all at once, and one more night and one more day and suddenly school resumed, work resumed, daily life resumed, and a strange spectre went about unseen.

In those days of red-booted freedom something black had come over the mountains: men in black uniforms and in plain clothes, civil servants, quiet people who went to work, grave and diligent, even as the pubs still echoed with cheering and song. They had set themselves up in a building next to the police station; there they worked, and certain people were summoned to the building where they worked, and we saw them go into the building, but we didn't see them come out, and at that we stopped looking so closely. Then came rumours that a certain person had been picked up and a certain person had managed to escape and a certain person was in a concentration camp now, but that didn't bother us, because certain people deserved to be picked up and sent to concentration camps: Commies, Social Democrats, Germans and Czechs alike, mostly workers, in short: the Commune. Quite right to go after them! But our conversations had turned quieter too, and we whispered more than we once had; Czech lessons were dropped, but in their place came racial theory and the history of the Prussian kings, we had to make up the material, cramming their wars and victories; the Reichenberg bank Father owed money had been

Aryanized, but the debts remained and grew still further as new, unexpected expenses arose: the taxes were higher, the Winter Relief Fund bluntly demanded tribute. The SA's* collecting boxes rattled, and I was in the SA too and had a collecting box to rattle, and people groaned when we came into the same cafe for the fifth time rattling the collecting box but our troop leader had ordered us to come back with a full box, and so we went into Café Neumann for the fifth and sixth and seventh time rattling our collecting boxes, and the people in the cafe, the tarock players, mariage players, billiard players, newspaper readers all groaned when we came to them for the fifth and sixth and seventh time rattling our boxes; they groaned, but they always reached into their pockets and took out their wallets and tossed coins into our collecting boxes, which still weren't full, for the SA's collecting boxes were deep with bulging sides. The people groaned, and here and there you heard, in whispers, the beloved old slogan reworded, now it went 'We want to go home from the Reich!' and here and there, in whispers, of course, people began to grumble that this wasn't what they'd pictured. Then came the great sell-out; travellers

---

* SA: Sturmabteilung, the paramilitary wing of the Nazi party until its purge in 1934. Also helped implement state-run charity drives.

from the Reich poured by the thousands across the
border that no longer was, and suddenly we found
all the restaurants and cafes and shops filled with
tourists who ate and drank and shopped and
couldn't get over how cheap things were over here.
I didn't understand it; Father had always com-
plained about the expensive times. Our senior
clerk, a dignified old gentleman with ink-stained
fingers, tried to explain it to me: the Czech crown
had had a very high purchasing power, he said,
which was completely out of proportion to the
official exchange rate of 1:8.6; wages and prices
had always been much lower here than in the Old
Reich, he explained, mentioning a price differen-
tial which used to be compensated by German
import taxes, and when he concluded that that was
why the Old Reich Germans could buy much
more in our parts than we could with our crowns,
and they'd soon buy us out of house and home if
it went on like this, I didn't understand any of it.
But it had to be true: every day a procession of
thousands came down from the mountains and
into our town, and they went to the shops and
bought a dress for three marks fifty and a pair of
men's shoes for two marks eighty and they sat in
the cafes and ate and drank, a glass of beer for ten
pfennigs, coffee with cake and whipped cream for
twenty pfennigs, and they ate and drank like we'd
never seen people eat and drink before. They'd

come up from Berlin and Hamburg and Leipzig
and even from the Rhineland; the trip had to pay
off, and so they sat in the cafes and devoured coffee
with cake and whipped cream for twenty pfennigs
and another portion and another and another and
got up and staggered to the toilet, Romans from
the Leine and the Pleisse, and stuck their fingers
down their throats and vomited, and then they
came back and went on eating and drinking,
twenty pfennigs a portion, and when they couldn't
choke down any more to save their lives they got
up and wobbled through the streets, heavy-laden
sloops, and clapped us on the shoulder and asked
if we were grateful they'd liberated us, and we said
yes, and they clapped us on the shoulder and said
we should be very grateful indeed, they'd spared
no sacrifice to liberate us and it was only right and
proper for them to take a little breather here and
have some coffee with cake and whipped cream,
they hadn't had that in the Reich in ages! Then
they hit the shops again and their bags filled with
shoes and silk stockings and lingerie and soap and
cigarettes and cookies and sardines and sausage
and Prague ham and watches and jewellery, and
then they hauled their bags over the border that no
longer was, and many of them stayed round and
set up shop. Many jobs had been freed up, positions once held by Jews and Reds, and so our liberators came and became mayor and judge and

district administrator and political director and
head of the Aryanized bank, and our senior clerk
said in a low voice that in the old days you'd had
to pay bribes to do well by yourself but the bribes
you had to pay these days, that was really over-
doing it. As he spoke he shook his head, the sparse
white hair flying about his temples, and then he
said in a hushed voice that the Führer didn't know
all the things that were going on, but soon he'd find
everything out, and then he'd clean house and
bring order and sweep out the Gau* with an iron
hand. His fingers trembled on the green blotter,
and I thought indignantly that you couldn't bother
the Führer with such trifles now: he was standing
at the controls of world history, and these were
serious times, Europe's rotten timbers were creak-
ing, everyone was asking anxiously whether there
would be war, you couldn't go to the Führer with
trifling business matters! And I said that to the
senior clerk, and he swayed his head and quietly
said that was true, the Führer had to save the Reich
from war now, and we both agreed that there was
only one man on earth who could do that, and that
was the Führer and the Führer alone.

---

* Gau: administrative region in Nazi Germany.

A WORLD WAR BREAKS OUT

1 September 1939,
Outbreak of the Second World War

It's strange, but I can't remember how I first heard that the Second World War had broken out: from my landlady or my classmates or the professors at my school—I no longer know. All the more strange as I recall the morning of that day quite clearly: awake early, I lolled in bed thinking over the questions the new school year would bring— 1 September was the first day of school—and these questions were many. For reasons of no interest here I had left Reichenberg and was now going to school in Hohenelbe, an insignificant little country town: I knew hardly any of my future classmates and teachers, so I pondered how best to make my entrance in the class, finally deciding to wear my SA uniform to school. As I recall, I did that in the end, but there my memories break off, and when I see myself next I'm sitting with my new classmates in the jam-packed auditorium, a hall like an amphitheatre hung with gaudy pictures, listening breathlessly to a Reichstag speech by the Führer that culminated in the words: 'As of 5:45 this morning, we are shooting back!'

After all that!

Even as the news of 'Polish atrocities against defenceless Germans which the Reich can no longer stand by and watch' multiplied in the papers, finally filling them entirely, I hadn't thought there would be war. When the Führer annexed the Protectorate* and the whole world spoke of war, war hadn't come, any more than it had when the Saar, Austria and the Sudetenland were annexed; why now, when the Führer was in the process of solving the Polish question and annexing Danzig, why now, of all times, should war break out? No, I hadn't thought of war, and my parents and my friends who winked at one another and whispered: 'Notice anything?' when new reports of atrocities came on the radio, they hadn't thought there'd be war either! The world would shriek, shriek with hate and envy and rage as always, but otherwise nothing would happen, and Danzig and the Warthegau would be annexed after all, in defiance of the enemies who begrudged us our *Lebensraum*! That was our thinking, and I remember the hours we spent brooding over maps and looking for more regions to annex: Danzig, the Corridor, Courland, the Warthegau,

---

* Protectorate: following the annexation of the Sudetenland, in March 1939, the majority-Czech remainder of Czechoslovakia was occupied by the German army, and the 'Protectorate of Bohemia and Moravia' was created.

the Memel Territory, East Upper Silesia, the Banat, Liechtenstein, German Switzerland, Alsatia, Eupen-Malmedy, Luxembourg, German Denmark, South Tyrol. Day after day we'd waited for a new annexation, and when the headlines of Polish atrocities exploded from the papers like cannon shots, we'd winked at one another and whispered: Now for Danzig and the Corridor! And we were convinced that once again it would work out peacefully; why, it had always worked out peacefully before!

But now, as of 5:45, we were shooting back, and the Führer was speaking in the Reichstag, and I remember that speech vividly. I thought it was superb: he, the Führer we trusted blindly, would follow blindly wherever he might lead, stepped before the Reichstag and rendered an account, which he owed to no one, of his stalwart efforts to salvage the peace; he set forth how he had wanted peace and only peace and nothing but peace and how he'd had only one single territorial demand left in Europe, and that was one single connecting road through the Corridor to East Prussia, and the Führer said that no German statesman but he could have made such a modest demand, anyone else would have been swept away by the people's wrath. Then the Führer spoke of the Polish atrocities against our defenceless brothers and sisters in the Warthegau, and outrage surged through the auditorium; we knew about atrocities against defenceless Germans, we'd had a taste of them ourselves. I thought of the barricades on the Reichenberg marketplace, and the border where the customs official had stolen our cigarettes, and all the bloody deeds we'd heard about on German radio, and now the Führer himself was speaking of the Polish atrocities, and he raised his voice and cried that despite it all he'd spent two whole days sitting with his cabinet in the Chancellery, waiting to see if the Poles would finally deign to send a representative to negotiate his last territorial demand. We heard this and marvelled at such long-suffering patience, and if someone had come and told us that the Polish ambassador in Berlin hadn't even been able to convey the German Chancellor's demands to Warsaw because his phone had been cut off for days, and if someone had told us that the outbreak of war had been set months ago to the day and hour and that the war had to be provoked because the Reich was bankrupt and that the Reich Chancellor had declared in so many words that he had but one fear, namely that some bastard might try to mediate at the last minute—if someone had come and told us that, we wouldn't even have torn him into pieces, we would have handed him over to a doctor as an obvious lunatic. No, what the Führer said was beyond the shadow of a doubt: for two whole days he'd sat waiting with his cabinet in the Chancellery to see if the Poles would finally deign to send a representative, and I pictured the Führer sitting for two days in the Chancellery with Göring and Goebbels and the other ministers I didn't know, waiting for the Polish representatives, and I saw a lofty hall, Gothic, Doric-columned, and in the middle of the hall, an enormous cross ending at the crossbeam, stood the negotiating tables: a line of massive ebony tables flanked by leather-padded ebony chairs with high backs and carved frames, and behind the crossbeam, on a raised seat, the Führer sat solemn-faced; to the right of the Führer, a bit lower, sat Field Marshal Göring; to the left of the Führer, at the same height as Göring, sat Goebbels, the Reich Propaganda Minister; round the vertical beam sat the other cabinet members whose names and faces I didn't know; and at the very end were two free chairs meant for Poland's representatives. Enormous chandeliers shed light on the solemn, silent hall, and the men sat silent at the tables and waited; the cabinet of the Greater German Reich sat there waiting, two whole days, forty-eight hours, but instead of sending representatives to Berlin, the Poles, we now heard, had whisked an armed band across the border, an armed band of soldiers in uniform whose ringleaders broke into the German radio station at Gleiwitz and shot at the ceiling and began talking Polish—that was Poland unmasked!

I didn't quite understand what good it did the Poles to break into the Gleiwitz radio station and shoot at the ceiling and talk Polish into the microphone, but finally I decided it must be a peculiarity of this obviously inferior race, and I burnt with outrage and agreed with the speaker: there was really nothing for it but to shoot back!

'As of 5:45 we are shooting back!' cried the Führer, and he cried that he'd only wanted peace and *Alljuda* wanted war, and now *Alljuda* had his war, the Führer cried, and once, I remember, we couldn't help laughing: the Führer blasted Roosevelt and his policy of peace guarantees and called him an old ninny, and we couldn't help laughing, and then the Führer said that the die of fate was cast, and suddenly I felt I was being sucked into a whirlpool, something bottomless, a cold, grey feeling, and quickly I thought to myself that the Führer would pull everything off all right, he'd always pulled it off before, and so he'd pull it off this time too, with the war and all, but I couldn't shake the grey, cold feeling. As if through cotton wool I heard Hitler say he had resolved to do his duty as an ordinary private from now until victory came, not doffing the people's honourable field-grey garb until the enemy lay shattered on the ground, and I thought to myself that now the Führer would join a regiment on the front as an ordinary private while Göring or Hess assumed leadership, and the grey feeling turned hollow, a hollow trepidation, and suddenly I decided to volunteer for the Wehrmacht. Now the Führer had ended his speech and we stood and shouted *Sieg Heil* along with the men in the Reichstag, then we sang the national anthem and the Horst Wessel Song, and then we stood awkwardly as the director, a fat little man in a frock coat with a medal from the World War on his chest, stepped forward and stammered in a faltering voice, clearing his throat several times, that after the Führer's deeply moving speech he simply had no words to express all that now stirred his soul and the soul of every good German man and boy, for the time of trials had come and all of us without exception would stand as one man behind our beloved Führer and follow him blindly wherever he might lead, and then he cleared his throat and told us that school was cancelled until further notice and new instructions would be given in due course, and then we all went home again, and it was war.

It was war, and we went home, and strange though it may sound, I remember little else that happened that day. Probably my memories have faded because after Hitler's speech everything was so different from what I'd imagined. It was war, the first day of the war, the die of fate was cast, and I thought something special had to happen now, a

special event, with a bang, a storm, the boom of
cannon, marching troops, cheering crowds; this
day had to unfold differently from the days before,
but there was nothing of the kind: no storm and
no bang, no cheering, no flowers, no flags, no
songs, a silent outbreak of war, a soundless cast
of the iron die; the men and women on the
streets looked scared, the mood was constrained,
depressed and depressing, and my mood must also
have been grey and uneasy. It was war, yet life went
on as it had always gone on before, and that was
suddenly ghostly, unreal: somewhere to the east
there was shooting and tanks and guns rolled and
soldiers fell and history marched with iron strides,
and in Hohenelbe the grocer sold salt and the
baker sold bread and the mailman delivered the
mail and the brewer's drayman rolled beer kegs,
and they all looked depressed and didn't talk
much, and suddenly I saw it as an absurd, even
criminal thing that the brewer's drayman was
rolling beer kegs now and the mailman delivering
mail and the baker selling bread and the grocer salt,
now that it was war, war, war, war! I thought that
now I too must act, and I ran to report to my SA-
Sturmführer, a white-haired captain of the former
Imperial and Royal Austro-Hungarian Army who
ran a real-estate business in Hohenelbe. The
Sturmführer was in uniform; he had put on his
medals and tramped up and down in his apartment

and smartly returned my smart salute. Then he
agreed with me that now we too must act; he
thought long and hard, and then he said that he
had no orders yet, but just in case, he was declaring
a red alert: every SA man must be in uniform and
at the ready, whether at home or at work. He
ordered me to pass on this message to the troop
leaders, and I ran to the troop leaders, who had
already put on their uniforms. Then I sat in my
room and listened to the news: victorious advance,
Führer at the front, Polish atrocities, English and
French threats, historic hour, and I know I slept in
my uniform and boots that night. The next morning school was still cancelled, and since it was a
Saturday I went home to my parents for the week-
end. I found them in a state of distress. 'I'm going
to volunteer,' I said, and my mother cried out, but
my father gave me a fearsome look and said: 'You
are not!'

'I'm going to volunteer,' I said, and my father,
thickset and strong as a bear, took my hands and
pressed them together and thrust me into an arm-
chair, saying, 'You are not!' and when I insisted on
volunteering my father shouted that he forbade
me, and if I went and did it in secret he'd go to the
draft registration office and publicly withdraw my
name—I was underage—even if it meant shaming
me before the world. I knew he would do it, and
said nothing more; slamming the door of my

room, I sat by the loudspeaker and listened to the news: victorious advance, Führer at the front, Polish atrocities, English and French threats, historic hour, and after the news came the reports from the propaganda units; the Führer ate pea soup in the field kitchen with his valiant soldiers and officers, the Field Marshal's wife tended the valiant wounded as an ordinary nurse; the government allotted the higher food rations to the heavy labourers and prohibited dances and other entertainment as long as our valiant soldiers were still falling at the front, and I thought with admiration that the Führer had pulled off the hardest thing of all: forming a community of the people and with it an army of the people in which general and soldier ate the same pea soup from the field kitchen and whose supreme commander was an ordinary private; and I resolved to volunteer after all despite my father's angry reaction. I sat by the radio and listened to the news and heard special reports of victories upon victories: Częstochowa captured, the Warta crossed east of Wieluń, the Jablunkov Pass seized, Polish airspace conquered and the strategic target of Warsaw bombed . . . I sat by the radio and heard of victories upon victories, and history marched with iron strides. All day long I didn't speak; my mother worked silently on blackout curtains for the bedroom; my father sat in the Rübezahl Tavern discussing the military situation, and that evening we met on the road and he took me by the hand and walked with me up towards the mountains a ways.

The windows of the houses were blacked out, not a light to be seen, the world lay black as a mine shaft, a dark cave roofed by the firmament. It was a stormy evening, grey and black clouds racing across the mountain summits; it was the Wild Hunt,* a rider, a riot of horses and hounds, and the Wild Hunt ran down the moon, a lemon-yellow crescent blazing above the peak. 'The old Jewish god's taking vengeance,' my father whispered. He had drunk a lot, but he stood unswaying, and he whispered softly, without slurring his words. 'The old Jewish god's taking vengeance,' he whispered, staring at the Wild Hunt as it carved up and wolfed down the moon. 'He's gone too far,' my father went on, 'he's gone too far, and now he'll drag us all down with him!'

I didn't understand what he was saying. I was afraid of him: was he raving? 'This time he'll drag the whole world in,' my father whispered and seized me by the shoulder and said: 'This is the World War, boy, Germany won't survive it!'

---

* The Wild Hunt: in German legend, an apparition of ghostly huntsmen headed by the god Odin; believed to presage war.

These words hit me like a blow from a club. 'But we have the Führer,' I stammered in utter confusion, and I said that there had never been another war in which the soldiers knew so clearly and surely what they were fighting for, and my father asked: 'Oh? What for, then?' and suddenly I had no answer to give and felt my heart begin to pound. It was dark, the storm raged, it had wolfed down the moon, and I heard its howling and cast about for an answer and found none and said something about honour and freedom, and felt even as I spoke that it was an empty phrase, and my father said that England and France would declare war on us tomorrow and America would follow, and that would be Germany's downfall. Suddenly he began to sway and slur his words; I grabbed him under the arms and took him home; darkness lay on the land like a sea, and I felt for the ground with my feet.

The next day—or wasn't it the next day?— England and France declared war on Germany, but I don't remember that day at all. Then school resumed and the radio reported victories upon victories, the armoured wedges advanced inexorably and with lightning speed, Warsaw was bombed and the Narew was crossed and England and France stayed put at the Siegfried Line without firing a shot, and we all saw the future in the rosiest of lights once more. 'Grand, the way our Führer's pulled it off again!' said my father, and there had never been any doubt that he might not pull it off. Half the class volunteered for the Wehrmacht, but they didn't take us: Germany had no need to wage its war with boys, said Major Glaser of the draft registration office, and so we went back to our books, and sixteen days later the Führer had pulled off Poland and annexed the Warthegau and East Upper Silesia and the Corridor and Danzig and the General Government* to the Reich, known since Austria's annexation as the Greater German Reich, and then the dancing ban was lifted, and we danced into the New Year at the Rübezahl Tavern. It was a glorious New Year's celebration with a flaming winter sun over the mountains, and then the Führer pulled off Denmark and Norway, and the dancing ban was back, and the Führer pulled off Belgium and Holland and France and Luxembourg and Yugoslavia and Greece and Crete and North Africa and the dancing ban was lifted again, but by that point the lifting of the dance ban did me no good; I had already joined the Reich Labour Service (RLS), and we were stationed on the Nemen, three kilometres from the Russian border, where there were no dance halls and no girls.

---

* General Government (Generalgouvernement): term under Nazi occupation for the region of Poland including Warsaw, Krakow and Lublin.

Our Reich Labour Service company had spent the past eight weeks stationed on the Nemen three kilometres from the German–Soviet border, believing, like all the soldiers round us whose barracks and tents and artillery covered the green rolling land in grey, that one day soon we would march straight through the Soviet Union to Persia or India, and there deal England the death blow. It was a long way from the Nemen to Teheran or to the Hindu Kush, but this mass concentration of troops could only mean deployment for action. The thinly settled green land was crammed with troops like a junk dealer's storeroom with scrap and rags; tanks, their mottled steel domes covered with alder boughs and reeds, stood like dinosaurs in the sparse woods; huge gasoline drums rolled day after day into underground bunkers; concrete runways were laid over open fields; columns of empty trucks parked beneath pollard birch crowns; and every day new units arrived and set up their tents and barracks. No doubt about it, we were in readiness, and since a treaty of friendship bound us to the Soviet Union, it could only be the march through to Persia or India. We labourers awaited our marching orders impatiently; since coming to the Nemen we'd had no meaningful work to do, following orders from our leaders, all of them shady characters and failures in civilian life, to shovel gravel rhythmically from one side to the other, dig away hills and raise them up elsewhere, lay railway tracks over log roads only to dismantle them the next day, glean stones from meadows and dig ditches in swampy ground that closed up overnight again, knock tight the shafts of our shovels and drill the goose step and knee bends against the clock, and we gazed enviously at all the sappers and artillerymen and infantrymen and flak gunners round us who led a glorious life by our standards: after duty they had free time and evenings out, while we were kept busy into the night and weren't allowed to leave the camp; their food was something from a fairy tale, and we barely got by on our monotonous fare; they got their service pay and we got our twenty-five pfennigs a day, and above all they were real soldiers, the nation's arms-bearers and all the girls' heartthrobs, while we carried no arms and the girls looked down their noses at us. Day after day brought the same drill and tedium, and we yearned for the advance as the day of our deliverance—at least we'd have some freedom, I thought; it would be easier to shirk duty now and then, we'd be monitored less strictly in our quarters, and above all we'd see something of the world: Lithuania and Latvia and White Russia and the Ukraine and the Don and the Caucasus, Baku and Tiflis, and finally the shimmering white Orient with its mosques and minarets and the mysteries of its seraglios and harems and bizarre bazaars; we'd see the world, I thought, the great wide world and not just the flat, green, rolling land of the past eight weeks with the one birch-lined path and the alder swamps and the bog beneath the hill on which our tents huddled, and the yellow gravel pit gaping like a dragon's maw where we lined up two by two day after day and shovelled gravel to one another with the prescribed arm movements, thinking longingly of the Peacock Throne and the dark temple of Kali. No, even a foot march to India couldn't be worse than these days on the Nemen. This had to be it, I thought.

As I recall, one of those days, a Saturday, got off to an especially bad start: at morning roll call we botched the 'eyes right', and the Feldmeister, a failed farmer from Windhoek, had us form groups of six instead of the usual eight to pick up the sections of railway track that were stacked in the corner of the parade ground, and then, deliberate and amused, counted off the eight beats of each of the fifty squats we had to perform with that crushing weight cutting into our hands. Willi, our weakest, collapsed; my hands bled afterwards, as did nearly all my comrades'; the medic came down the line daubing the broken skin with iodine, and the Feldmeister stood on the parade ground with arms akimbo and bobbed up and down and shouted that we shouldn't even think of getting time off, much less going out this afternoon or tomorrow on Sunday, he'd work us so hard we wouldn't dream of a woman (he put it a bit more crudely) for the next three months. Then we marched down to the gravel pit on the double, singing, and lined up two by two and began shovelling; six hours in, the day was already hot, and I thought of noon with dread. My hands burnt, and I could hardly hold the shovel any more when a messenger came running from the orderly room and brought the Feldmeister a message, and the Feldmeister looked at his watch, and then he ordered: 'Stop work!' and had us form ranks, and we marched back. There were no dirty tricks on the way back. This is it, this is it, I thought.

No question, this was it: first-aid kits were handed out and steel helmets and two tins of meat and a pack of biscuits as an iron ration and then, to our great surprise, bicycles, brand new, brown-painted bicycles, and the troop leader who handed out the brand new, brown-painted bicycles laughed and asked if any of the men didn't know how to ride a bike, because he'd have an hour to teach them, but it turned out everyone did know how to ride a bike, and we were ordered to mount and mounted and rode a ways down the path, happy that we were going to ride through the world on bicycles and wouldn't have to march, and we rode to a depot near the gravel pit and parked our bicycles there, and the Feldmeister, who had ridden in front of us on a touring cycle, ordered us to enter the depot six by six. I was among the first six to enter. I stepped inside the depot and thought my heart would stop. In the depot, on wooden racks, lay rifles.

Rifles, my god, these were rifles, real rifles, unbelievable, and I thought we'd only come here to transport the rifles someplace else, but then our names were called and one by one, I was the fourth, we stepped up to a counter in front of the wooden racks, and one by one we received our rifles, real rifles, the kind real soldiers carried, Carbine 98k, and five rounds of live ammunition, and for the first time I held a real rifle in my hands and cradled it and felt its weight, and then we signed in a notebook and went back out with the rifles in our hands and our comrades stared at us incredulously, and then the next six were called up and went into the shed and came back out again with rifles in their hands, and we all had rifles, real rifles, and I tore open the trigger lock and looked down the barrel, the long, shiny, steel rifle barrel, and round me all my comrades cradled the rifles in their hands and tore open the trigger locks and looked down the barrels and the sky was nothing but a tiny pale circle above a vast steel spiral, and then we shut the locks again and now, good god, the rifles were cocked, and we looked down the sights and suddenly the tree we saw no longer had branches and leaves, just points to align the notch and bead with; the whole world had become one great bull's-eye, and the Feldmeister yelled: 'Not at one another, you loons!' and we stared at our rifles and memorized the rifle number, and then we slung the rifles over our shoulders and mounted our bicycles and rode back to the parade ground and drilled: 'Shoulder arms!' and 'Present arms!' and it was the first fun drill we'd had. The Feldmeister actually praised us and said the good drill had made up for the fiasco that morning, and then we rode to the shooting range and shot at the target with live ammunition, and I shot two sevens and one nine and made the cut and was a happy man. The day flew past; we packed our knapsacks and sent home the things we didn't need and polished our bicycles and oiled our rifles, and then we rode back to the shooting range and shot at a human form: chest, head and helmet, and we hit the chest and the head and the helmet, and in the evening as we sat dead tired on our packed knapsacks and argued about whether we were marching to Persia or India, an iron rail was struck like a gong, and Eugen, our foreman, yelled: 'Gas!' and we pulled the gas masks over our faces and raced outside. There had been plenty of gas alerts since we'd pitched camp on this hill above the bog; one of the officers' favourite and nastiest tricks was to call a gas alert and make us double-time and sing and crawl with the gas mask filters screwed tight, but this time it was no trick: the Feldmeister motioned us to surround him in a semicircle, and said in a hushed voice that everyone should make sure his gas mask was airtight, this wasn't a game any more, it was a matter of life and death; the Russkis were capable of anything, even using gas. I thought I hadn't heard right. 'The Russkis are capable of anything, they'll even use gas,' said the Feldmeister. We stared at one another through the round windows of our gas masks. The Russians then, the Russians! It was already dark; below, at the edge of the bog, a troop leader was burning stacks of documents; I saw the crackling red flames and the black pools amid the grasses reflected their glow and the smoke of the charring paper drifted past us with the weak west wind, but we didn't feel it, we had gas masks over our faces, their rubber hugging cheeks and chin. It was the Russians then, the Russians! The fires crackled; bubbles swelled in the bog. We stood without a word. Suddenly it occurred to me that today was Midsummer Night, the solstice, the shortest night after the longest day. The fires sprayed sparks. The border lay three kilometres, four thousand marching paces away. Then it was the Russians, the Russians after all! Beneath the gas mask my breath came fast: we're marching against Russia! Suddenly everything was clear to me: we had to go up against Russia!

As I vividly recall, the signing of the German–Soviet Non-Aggression Pact was the first time I doubted the rightness of the Führer's policies. Providence had sent him to wipe out Bolshevism and destroy it root and branch, and now he was making pacts with the heartland of Bolshevism, the Soviet Union, that Satanic state, that empire of thieves, whores and criminals. How could that be? I hadn't understood, and my father was unable to explain it to me; I hadn't understood, and then, as we prevailed on all fronts, I had forgotten the question, but now suddenly it seemed to be solved: the Führer completed his mission, a Gordian knot was severed with a sword stroke, we went up against Bolshevism, Europe's elite against the hordes of Asia, the eternal Catalaunian Battle* was drawing

---

* Catalaunian Battle: in 451 CE the Huns were defeated by a Roman-Visigoth force in the Battle of the Catalaunian Plains.

to an end, and I didn't doubt for a moment that we would emerge as victors from a terrifying struggle. Catalaunian Battle; the armies swept through the air, Siegfried against Attila, the Nibelungs against Genghis Khan; the die of fate rolled, the world's most historic hour thundered up: tomorrow the destruction of Bolshevism would begin, a new epoch of world history had dawned, and we'd been there from the very first minute and held our rifles in our hands and the gas masks covered our mouths and eyes and the Feldmeister said: 'Take care, men, and go to sleep now, tomorrow you'll need your strength!' and we took off the gas masks and said: 'Yes, sir!' and then we went to our tents and laid our heads on our packed knapsacks, and I thought I wouldn't be able to sleep that night, but I was dead tired and dropped off quickly.

I had no dreams; we were woken at three; it was a pallid morning, with stars still out, and the moon, a stroke of silver, hung low. We fell in; there was a quick roll call, then we hunkered down on our knapsacks and drank a cup of coffee and ate bread with syrup and then we waited. We spoke little and smoked cigarette after cigarette; for an hour and a half we hunkered like that on our brown knapsacks, rifles slung over our shoulders, and smoked and gazed over to the east, to the border over which, slow in a red steam, the sun rose into a cloudless sky. The sky turned red, Catalaunian

Battle, and all at once I recalled a poem by Georg Heym:

> Arisen is he who long lay asleep,
>
> Arisen from vaults deep underneath.
>
> Huge and unknown in the dawn he stands,
>
> And he crushes the moon between his black hands ...

and I thought to myself that the war thus far with its lightning victories in Poland and in the west and the north and the south hadn't yet been a real war but now this war against the Bolsheviks would be one such as the world had never known, and I saw the war standing huge and unknown on the horizon, half charburner, half hoplite, black, on his skull the helmet with the horsehair crest, and I saw him reach for the moon and crush the moon in his hands, and I tried to remember the next stanzas, but recalled only one more line: a great city sank in yellow smoke—and the sun broke away from the horizon and rose into the sky and the sky began to thunder. Catalaunian Battle, the sky thundered, a bomber squadron swept down the sky and into the flaming morning sun. It swept steadily in rank and file, as though it were on parade; the steel wings thrummed, the propellers' white circles flashed. I looked at my watch; it was half past four; so this was the historic hour when the destruction of Bolshevism began: four-thirty, the first summer

day, the first Sunday in summer, and I was there!
The bombers had passed, thunder echoed from
the border, the air thrummed: Catalaunian Battle!
We hunkered on our knapsacks and waited and all
round the land was on the march; we waited feverishly till nearly noon; our stomachs growled, we'd
smoked our last cigarettes and heard the tanks
churn and the planes drone and waited and our
stomachs growled, and just as food was about to
be served the order came to depart and we rode
down the birch-lined path we'd always marched
along to the gravel pit and rode past the gravel pit
and suddenly everything was forgotten, the drill,
the polish, the dirty tricks, the hunger, everything:
we were in action now and rolling towards the
enemy! The path led to an asphalt road, and here
we had to wait again: columns of trucks rolled
down the road and blocked our way, truck after
truck, gigantic processionary caterpillars, and behind the trucks rolled an anti-aircraft battalion and
then came trucks again with soldiers on them and
then the way was finally clear and we rode. We
rode in march formation, three men abreast, one
long column; we rode and left and right lay green
rolling land; by the road stood silver thistles;
ditches gleamed; alders and willows; suddenly the
asphalt road narrowed, on the ground lay splintered wood, was that the border? Already past; we
rode along, the land lay green and rolling, here and

there tank treads had torn up the asphalt, and then a dead goat lay in the grass, a dead goat, snow-white, its legs stretched up into the sky, a rune of death carved out white in the land. It stank; we rode past; craters in the green, spilt earth; a burnt-out truck, empty gasoline drums, alder woods in the background: so this was already enemy land, Eastland, conquered ground! Brown heaps lay in the grass off to the side. Were those dead people? Graves? Where was the enemy? An infantry platoon marched down the road ahead of us; their faces were tired, their steps already leaden, they must have been marching since early that morning and couldn't catch up with the front. At their head strode a lieutenant in ice-grey, wiping the sweat from his brow; 'Column from the left!' the cry came down the platoon, and the lieutenant shouted: 'Move right!' and the infantry stood aside, really and truly, they made way for us, and we rode past, our rifles on our backs, and then we had to make way, a tank column passed us, and then came the first village, poor farmsteads, deserted, half-timbered buildings roofed with reeds and shingles. One house had been shelled, dust rose from the ruins. We wanted to go to the well, but the Feldmeister wouldn't let us; he said the water might be poisoned. The sun beat down, we rode on, thirsty, and again flights of bombers passed and again the ground and the air shook.

The village fell behind; the alder woods closed in on the road, which began to climb, and at the top of the hill a bomb crater had destroyed the asphalt surface.

The Feldmeister had us dismount to fix the road; we got off our bicycles and were beginning to fill in the craters when a small procession came up the hill from the other side, soldiers in tattered olive-brown uniforms; they walked wearily and hung their heads and their skulls were shaved and their faces grey with dust and sweat and exhaustion. An older private escorted them, a rifle with a fixed bayonet tucked under his arm. They dragged themselves along, and one pulled a small gun on wheels behind him; his head was bound, and the bandage was crusted with blood. 'Poor devil,' said Willi, shovelling beside me, and gave the man a pitying look as he stumbled on, but the Feldmeister overheard and snarled at Willi and said that Bolsheviks deserved no pity, and only then did we actually realize those were Bolsheviks, enemies, criminals, and we lowered our shovels and stared at them open-mouthed and the Feldmeister repeated that *Untermenschen* deserved no pity: we could see for ourselves how they shambled along with their slanty eyes and high cheekbones and shaved skulls, an Eastlandish Slavic Mongol mishmash, simply insupportable, racially speaking, and we saw it for ourselves: slanty eyes and high cheekbones and shaved skulls, those just had to be *Untermenschen*! The column vanished from our sight. Now, we Germans were the masters here for all time, the Feldmeister said, and bobbed up and down, and he said that we must show no pity, they'd just take that as a sign of weakness, and we nodded and went on shovelling with hands that still burnt from the iodine-daubed wounds, and then we rode on again into the land that was now conquered ground. My gullet was parched, my stomach growled, and the rifle weighed heavy on my shoulders; with an aching back I pedalled mechanically and my only thought was not to fall behind. Then suddenly traffic stalled and we were wedged between columns of trucks and motorcycles; it seemed a bridge had been dynamited and was being repaired, and we staggered from the road and fell into the grass and stretched out our legs and waited without speaking, and I felt sick with hunger, when suddenly the columns began moving again, and the Feldmeister cursed because we took too long moving our bicycles into the rolling flood and made no headway, and I heard him curse yet without really hearing him, and at last we found an opening, and I pedalled mechanically with just one fear, that I'd fall by the wayside, and we rode along and it was evening already and I thought I'd fall by the wayside after all, when we turned onto a side road and came to a village, and the Feldmeister ordered us to stop and dismount and said that our first march objective had been reached and we would take up quarters here. The scattered houses all seemed unoccupied: no human face to be seen, no human voice to be heard, and we heard no animal sounds but the buzzing of mosquitoes in the steamy evening air. We stacked the rifles and bicycles together and waited; the Feldmeister and his staff vanished behind the nearest house and we stood in the middle of the marketplace and suddenly I thought this was all just a dream: one moment the noise of the motors and the sputter of exhaust and the cursing of the drivers and the babble of commanding voices and now not a sound and we stood in enemy land and hadn't fired a shot yet and early that morning we'd been sitting on a hill on the Nemen smoking cigarettes and drinking hot coffee and now we were standing here in a Lithuanian village and clouds drifted in the sky, little clouds, and mosquitoes buzzed, and then a troop leader came and motioned us to follow him and assigned us quarters in one of the farmhouses.

We entered through a porch and suddenly stood in a large parlour where just that morning the occupants had sat at the table eating breakfast: dishes were still on the table and knives and forks and a salt cellar, and unwashed pots on the stove, and we opened the door to the next room and there stood two beds, heavy oak furniture without blankets or pillows, and a wardrobe stood there, an emptied wardrobe, and the troop leader ordered us to take the beds over to headquarters so there'd be room here for all of us, and we stood awkward and helpless in this strange house that was now our quarters, still suffused by the breath of its previous owners. I looked round and saw in the corner an image of the Virgin, a blue Virgin with the Infant in her arms, and I didn't understand all this. Why, God was banned in Bolshevik Russia, and anyone who believed in him was shot by the Cheka,* that had been in the newspaper hundreds of times, and now the image of the Virgin hung in the corner smiling at us, a blue Virgin with a golden halo, and in her arms the naked Baby Jesus smiled too. Under the image of the Virgin ran a wooden shelf with paper-bound books; I wanted to leaf through them, but didn't dare as long as the troop leader was still round, and so I took my knapsack and carried it into the room where the beds had been, and the troop leader stood in the parlour under the image of the Virgin and assigned people to guard duty and kitchen duty and a number of other work details such as latrine builder and messenger and then he went away again and I'd been lucky: I got

---

* Cheka: Soviet secret police

off scot-free. The work details set off, grumbling; we untied our knapsacks and unstrapped the blankets and tarps and laid them out on the floor and I thought of the Feldmeister's words, that we were the masters here now, and I resolved to be a good and gentle master.

I meant to be a gentle master: I had dreamt of Russia ever since devouring Dostoyevsky's novels at the age of fifteen. They captured all the wild, confused, contradictory emotions and mental tempests of my adolescence: rebellion and perplexity, ferment and outcry and tormenting questions of crime and punishment and guilt and redemption; they had a mystery that could never fully be interpreted; and by the time I'd seen a film of Pushkin's 'Postmaster' and heard one of the White Cossack choirs, Russia had become the land of my heart, of course a Russia without Bolsheviks, sacred, old Mother Russia with its barbaric peasants and Volga boatmen and the unfathomable soul dreaming in gold spires and Cossack choirs and white onion domes which had brought forth Little Father Tsar and the monk Rasputin and Raskolnikov and the prophet Luka, God's messenger in the Lower Depths, that sacred soul which had been gagged by the Bolsheviks and thrown into the dungeon where it cried out for freedom, as I knew from Rakhmanova's* memoirs, and I thought to myself that we would bring the ancient sacred Russian soul its freedom, and I resolved to be a good master to the Russians. Meanwhile we had unrolled our blankets and tarps and stood round in the parlour listening to our stomachs growl, and then someone said we should go look for straw, and with some hesitation, not knowing if it was allowed, we left the house and went over to the barn, and there was straw, big bales of straw, and we took the straw and carried it to our quarters and spread the straw out on the floor and from all the rooms our comrades came and carried straw and others carried water and wood to the field kitchen, and steam began to rise from the field kitchen and suddenly it smelt of fried potatoes. The smell drugged me; I hadn't eaten fried potatoes since joining the Labour Service and now it smelt of fried potatoes, richly pervasive, but the smell of fried potatoes didn't come from the field kitchen; there barley simmered in a murky liquid. The smell of fried potatoes came from the house where our staff had taken up quarters; we went over and saw a troop leader standing at the stove frying potatoes

---

*Alya Rakhmanova (real name Galina Dyuragina, 1898–1991): her extremely popular memoirs, published in the 1930s, described the suffering of her aristocratic family under the Bolshevik regime.

in an enormous skillet of sizzling oil, and I was wondering where the troop leader had got the oil when Eugen, our foreman, grabbed my arm and said: 'Hey, they just went and organized it!'

I asked what we should do and Eugen said we should go organize something too; I couldn't quite picture what that meant, but Eugen said that first we should get our rifles and then head out, and the rest was sure to follow. So we fetched our rifles and searched the house next door; like our quarters, it had been abandoned by its occupants; the kitchen and pantry had been cleaned out, the yard was empty and straight across it in the sand ran a trail of blood and chicken feathers lay in one corner. 'Someone got here before us,' said Eugen, and suddenly he slapped his forehead and ran to the cellar of our quarters and rattled at the cellar door. The door was locked, so we battered the panels with our rifle butts, and as the wood of the panels began to splinter we heard voices from the cellar and the door opened from inside and out came, hands raised, the farmer and his wife, old people, white-haired, fear etched with steel on their furrowed faces.

'We won't hurt you,' said Eugen, 'we just want a little butter, understand? Butter and bacon and a few potatoes!' but the old people didn't understand a thing, they listened fear-racked to the incomprehensible foreign sounds and stared at our swastika armbands, and Eugen repeated, 'Butter, understand?' and 'Bacon and potatoes!' I said, but the two looked at one another helplessly.

'Butter, damn it, don't you understand?' Eugen said angrily and tucked his rifle between his legs and held out the palm of his left hand as if it were a slice of bread and made a buttering motion with his right hand and repeated: 'Butter, capeesh?' and I said 'Bacon!' and made the motion of slicing bacon and put the imaginary piece of bacon in my mouth and began chewing and the two old people shook their heads and the farmer said: 'Nix, nix,' and suddenly his wife was talking to us urgently and gripping my hand and there were tears in her eyes. 'Out of the way!' said Eugen and pushed them aside, and we climbed down the narrow stairs to the cellar and saw that this cellar had nothing more to offer: hooks hung empty of sausages and hams, the baskets were empty and the barrels pried open; there was a heap of clothes and bedding in one corner, but we weren't interested in that.

'There's nothing here worth taking,' I said, but Eugen said the little beggars must have buried it or hidden it somehow, and we searched the cellar for signs of digging but found none, and Eugen said if you just held your rifle to the Red vermin's chests and played round with the trigger, the little beggars would cough up the sides of bacon soon enough, and the tubs of butter and the hams. I wasn't so happy with the idea; I wanted to be a good master, after all, but I didn't want to embarrass myself in front of Eugen, and Eugen poked the farmer in the chest with the rifle barrel and said: 'Cough up the stuff, where'd you hide it?' The farmer's hands trembled and he said 'Nix' and his voice choked; his wife covered her face with her hands and cried out, and then she lowered her hands from her face and grabbed our sleeves and began talking with feverish, imploring haste, and I felt sorry for her, but I thought to myself that there was a war on, after all, and in every war the farmers have to feed the soldiers, and Eugen waved the rifle barrel round and now everywhere all the houses and cellars were breached with guns and rifle butts and the farmers came out of their hiding places and raised their hands and we were nineteen years old and had rifles and twenty rounds of live ammunition and everywhere came cries for butter and bacon and sausage and bread, when a whistle shrilled out in the tumult. The troop leader stood in the middle of the marketplace blowing the whistle and shouting red-faced: 'Fall in!' and we fell in and the troop leader yelled at us, asking if we'd lost our minds; we were to hightail it to our quarters and stay out of the other houses; it wasn't our job to find provisions, and the other quarters were designated for the Wehrmacht! He yelled a bit longer, and then he shooed us back to our quarters and we looked out the window at the Staff HQ and saw the officers sitting round the table piling fried potatoes onto their tin plates, and we all agreed that this was a scandal that could only happen in the RLS. Then night came, and then the Wehrmacht, an artillery division with horse-drawn guns, and they settled in and again the cellar doors splintered and again the farmers came out and the soldiers held up their rifles and then suddenly all round there was a smell of fried potatoes and chicken, and we each ate our ladleful of grey barley with a few shreds of meat and chewed a piece of dry bread, and then we searched our quarters again from attic to cellar, but found nothing edible. There was a pile of half-charred wood in the yard, and we poked round in it; maybe someone had been roasting potatoes and there'd still be some left, but it was only half-charred wood which must have had writing on it, a few fragments still decipherable: 'rman comra' and 'lay dow' and 'worke nd farme' and we left the pile of wood alone and turned to go, disappointed. The artillerists had a loudspeaker they'd put in the open window, and we listened to march music and then the news: at the very last minute, said the newscaster, the Führer had pre-empted the bloody Bolsheviks' imminent attack on Europe, dealing a devastating blow to the Red Army's obvious deployment for attack, and the newscaster said that now the final, decisive battle against Bolshevism had broken out and our brave troops had overrun the enemy along the entire front, hurling him back as far as a hundred kilometres in places, and the tank spearheads were pressing inexorably forward, said the speaker, inexorably forward like a knife through butter, and I thought of how we'd pressed inexorably forward too, even though we were only RLS and riding bicycles, and I thought to make a careful note of everything so that I could tell the regulars at the Rübezahl Tavern how it all had happened.

'In eight weeks it'll all be over,' said Eugen, 'you can count on it!' and I said in eight weeks we might be entering Moscow already, and the marches blared through a night that blazed with stars; the marches blared and it smelt of fried potatoes and then a fairy-tale voice sang Tosca's aria and the night was still and the stars blazed like crown jewels. A horse neighed wildly. 'Man, in Moscow we'll stuff ourselves with caviar,' said Eugen, 'that's where those Red bigwigs keep all the caviar and vodka, for sure,' and the loudspeaker blared and there was a rushing in the air, Catalaunian Battle, and then a radiant tenor sang the Meistersinger's song, and I stood with Willi at the window gazing out into the night, and Eugen said,

'Man, hopefully we'll be in the Wehrmacht by the time we march into Moscow, and not in the shitty Labour Service!'

When German radio reported that Moscow would fall any hour now, we were packing to march to the Oppeln station from where we'd take the train east to be deployed. I was in the RLS no longer, I'd got lucky: past Narva I'd incurred an inguinal hernia while building log roads; the hernia became strangulated, putting my life at risk, and had to be operated on, so I had been admitted to a homeland military hospital and ten days later, following a successful operation and recovery, was transferred to the Wehrmacht. As I was still considered convalescent I was assigned to light duty with a teletype company of the air signal corps which, after half a year of training, would now be deployed in the east. On 9 December, five weeks before my twentieth birthday, we'd boarded the overheated train to Kiev; the journey, spent dozing by day and playing cards by night as the train sped through wastes of snow, had taken six days, and now we were sitting in the headquarters of the Ukraine Air Signal Regiment, a former school in Kiev, waiting for our company commander, who was receiving his operational orders from the regimental commander. It was warm in the classroom where we sat waiting, and we lolled luxuriously on the school benches. Outside it was forty-four below, and the wind swung its axe at every corner; it had sliced through our thin linen coats in no time as we marched from the train station to headquarters, and halfway there Alfred, next to me, stared and said aghast that my nose was white, and I stared at him and said that his nose had turned white too, like a cauliflower stalk, and then we rubbed our noses and cheeks with snow until they turned flaming red, hardly able to hold the snow in fingers that had gone numb despite the gloves, stiff as ebonite rods. The white frost had spared no one's nose and cheeks; it had been a punishing march, but now we sat on the comfortable benches in the heated room and stretched out our legs and dozed. Through drooping lids I saw the light-yellow room, decorated with stucco shells and fruit; I stretched my limbs and wondered where and how I would be deployed and hoped I could stay in Kiev: even with frost-burnt eyes I'd seen, enthralled, the city's splendour—never had I seen a city crowned with gold! Ah, crowned with gold, you'd have to see it in summer, I thought, crowned with gold and flower-suns swaying round it and July blazing on its domes and towers! Crowned with gold-and-blue onion domes, patina and six golden crosses above the cathedral's aquamarine, the pillars' snowy marble: that was Kiev, and when Nature smiled it had to be a dream of a city. I got up and gazed out the window, but out the window there was little to see: an icy courtyard where trucks froze, skeletons of trees, red and green fences and a statue's pedestal with no statue on it. I gazed out the window, and suddenly felt tired; I thought of taking a nap; the meeting would probably drag on and I could catch fifteen minutes of sleep before I had to go back out into the cold. Some of my comrades were already asleep, others were playing cards or smoking or dozing or reading trashy novels. There was little conversation.

I sat back down on the bench and dozed. It was warm; the wall and the stucco swam before my eyes, and then, half asleep, I saw green domes and a blue wooden gate from which a bearded peasant suddenly rose into the air. One hand was buried in his beard, and the other hand held a fiddle with a bird's head; I wondered, dozing off, where I had seen this image before, and after the peasant trotted a cow with a transparent belly and a calf inside, blue, pale, a pale-blue calf, and suddenly the door burst open, the floor shook, and I started up. A major stood at the door with a telex in his hand; brusquely waving away the first sergeant who jumped up to report, he shouted breathlessly: 'Is

Colonel Bronner here?' and the first sergeant stood at attention and shouted: 'No, Sir!' and the major turned and ran down the corridor. The first sergeant forgot to call 'Attention'; he stared after the major, and we stared after the major too: a major running, we'd never seen anything like it. Even the sleepers had woken with a start. 'What's going on?' one asked, but no one could give him an answer. The first sergeant shook his head in disbelief. The major had disappeared round the bend in the corridor. 'Colonel von Bronner!' a voice yelled behind the wall. We saw the city through the corridor window. A door opened with a bang; a sergeant ran out; the first sergeant called to him, but the sergeant didn't hear him and ran down the corridor. From the open door came the shrill ring of a field telephone. 'Sit back down, men!' said the first sergeant, and it seemed to me, absurd though it was, that his voice had a pleading ring. We stayed standing in the corridor. It was utterly still. 'Men,' said the first sergeant, and then said nothing more. I had a strange feeling: empty, like hunger that has passed. Icicles hung outside the window. We looked at one another helplessly. Something unspeakable had to happen. But nothing did.

We stood in the corridor waiting. Nothing.

Nothing happened.

Nothing happened: the icicles hung outside the window, thick glassy ice shot with blue; muffled forms darted across the street, a corpse hung from a balcony, the corridor was empty, with barely an echo of the shouts and running feet; the shrill ringing had fallen silent; clouds drifted, cigar fumes and gouts of smoke from pipes; it was warm and the benches in the classroom stood unmoved. Nothing had happened, what could possibly have happened, everything was completely normal, we were stationed in Kiev waiting for the operational orders that would assign us to one of the airports in Kiev, Poltava, Kharkov, Dnepropetrovsk, Stalino or Zaporozhye, or to one of the big signal centres in Kiev, Kharkov or Poltava. Ah, Kiev, Kiev, cradle of the Tsars, gold-crowned city mirroring its own patina, could I but linger as a guest in your walls! I went back to my bench and suddenly a name came to mind: Marc Chagall. Unsure what to make of this name, its strange taste upon the tongue like an exotic dish, I recalled my daydream: blue towers, green domes, and the bearded peasant rising over them, and remembered now where I had seen this image: in a history of modern art my father had won as fourth prize in the charity raffle at the 1937 Beach Festival in Roditz. A spa guest had forgotten the book at the Rübezahl Tavern, and so it ended up in the Beach Festival charity raffle; though my father, when he won it, joked that he would have preferred the fifth prize, a bottle of champagne, this picture had fascinated me like none before it.

Oh, the pale-blue calf in the cow's belly, the Holy
Mother of Cattle, and all at once I saw the Beach
Festival: the muddy pond in the grass, hemmed by
alder planks, round it tents and booths on fresh-
strewn gravel; it was illuminated, with bobbing
lanterns and pennants, and people sold sausages
and potato salad and vanilla ice cream and coffee
and beer and corn schnapps; Hansl Jaksch played
the accordion, Adolf Dohnt played the fiddle, and
Wenzel Votrubetz, jolly Wenzel from Seiffersdorf,
beat the drum, and there was dancing on a plat-
form of rough planks; a jasmine bush and Hanna,
god, how far back was that, I'd held her hand so
long in mine and the lanterns glowed, glow-worms
flickering, glimmering, twilight all round, just
lanterns glowing, and Sacher the dentist jumped
into the water in his black suit to impress his
beloved, Frau Motzel, who owned the Rübezahl
Tavern, and we laughed and Frau Motzel shrieked
and we dragged him soaked from the water, soaked
through and through, and then came the high
point of the evening: the sinking of the Titanic!
Glow-worms over the water, the Titanic slicing the
sea, and suddenly a blast: green and blue and purple and red, and the boat burst apart in the water,
broken through instantly, everything happened
instantly, powder smoke roiled, rockets shot up,
sprayed over the mountains purple-blue, broken
through, he said, and the Titanic spun, the bench

tipped, it couldn't be true, broken through, what, broken through, a red hole, a hammering in the brain: broken through, broken through, broken through; I staggered to my feet, the voice echoing: broken through, broken through, and we were running down the corridor, the walls stared white, white walls all round, the corridor shook, broken through, O words of thunder! We ran down the corridor, all I saw was white walls and heard: broken through, over and over those words of thunder: broken through, and then suddenly we were crowded together in the auditorium, and an officer was speaking, a colonel, I believe. I remember little of what he said, all I heard was: broken through, and the colonel said that the Russians had broken through near Moscow; it was their last desperate breakthrough, he said, but all I heard was: broken through, and the colonel said it was General Winter playing tricks on us: the winter made no difference to the Russians, said the Colonel, they were used to it as *Untermenschen*, but it made a big difference to us, he said, because it didn't get this cold in Germany, and that was why the Russians had broken through now, said the Colonel, but it was the last swipe of the paw from a mortally wounded predator, he said, and his words echoed in the whitewashed hall. A chill ran through me: never yet, I thought, had an enemy broken through German lines, not in the World War, when we'd gone unvanquished in the field, and in this war *we* were the ones who'd broken through everywhere, through the Polish Westerplatte and through the Maginot Line and through the English blockade and through the Greek mountain fortifications and through the Red Army's barriers and just this morning the radio had reported that we'd soon break through the last defensive ring round Moscow, and now a Russian breakthrough, that just couldn't be! I looked round, the whitewashed walls and the white ceiling and great growths of ice outside the window: General Winter was in command; we'd had to rub our nose and ears with snow on the march from the train station to here, and the infantry on the front lay in foxholes, outside, outside Moscow, in foxholes, and suddenly I stopped hearing what the colonel was saying. I felt a faraway hand close on my throat, I felt it vividly, cutting off the air, the walls were white, snow-white, we were sitting in an ice-house, the whole Wehrmacht was sitting in a giant ice-house; what did we want outside Moscow, what were we doing in Kiev, it was madness, even Napoleon hadn't been able to pull it off! I thought of Napoleon now, not the Führer: he'd made it into Moscow, and then Moscow had burnt, and there was a river there, what was it called, Brennesiva, no, that wasn't it; where was that, it had to be past Kiev, right? And what if it was all just a huge trap? What if the Russians had only tricked us by letting us up to Moscow, what if their main force now flanked us: to the north near Leningrad and to the south in the Caucasus and to the east near Moscow and at our rear the Poles and the Czechs, and now it went click, and the trap, the most ingenious trap in world history, snapped shut? Up front someone was talking, what was the point, we had to get out of here, the trap was snapping shut, a major had gone running, why didn't we jump onto the trucks and drive away, back where General Winter couldn't come, to the Reich, to the border, we'd fend off the *Untermenschen* there, where it wasn't forty-four below, shuddering down the front from Finland to the Crimea!

I recall little of what happened after that. All I know is that we moved the benches out of the classroom and bedded down in the empty room, and that we used straw mattresses: whitish grey mattresses slit in the middle, two of them making a bed for three. But before we went to sleep, and I still see it vividly before me, I took from my knapsack a little calendar I wrote poems in and carefully unfolded a piece of paper that was creased eight times and tucked behind a strip of canvas. It was a map of the world, 1:100,000,000; I had never looked at the map before, having hated geography ever since school, but now I unfolded it carefully and looked at the Earth's eastern half. I wanted to

see where the Berezina, now I had the name, where
the Berezina was, before Kiev or beyond it, but I
couldn't find the Berezina. Kiev, though, I found
at once: it was the city at the outermost western
rim of a vast red realm by which a few coloured
dots clustered, one of them called Germany. I
stared at the map and couldn't believe my eyes: we
had advanced for months inexorably, like a knife
through butter, yet we'd parted no more than the
skin of an apple! There lay the Russian realm, red,
Soviet Russia; it spanned half the Earth, not beginning in earnest until the Urals, and then came the
Amur and there lay Siberia and Kazakhstan, the
Lena and Cape Chelyuskin and Chita and the
Pamir and at the very left, the very rim, the western
rim, lay Kiev, a mere scratch to get that far, a
scratch in Heracles' skin. The Berezina wasn't
shown; I stared at the map and suddenly I had to
think of how I wanted to go to the university and
study philosophy and German literature and jour-
nalism, I wanted to be a journalist and follow the
times as they unfolded and write poems and rumi-
nate on the cosmos and now I hunkered on a mat-
tress in Kiev staring at a map and on the map was
a vast realm and that realm was red. Suddenly I
thought to myself that now we had to fight. Give
us machine guns! I thought, give us hand grenades,
flamethrowers, cannons, we have to get out there
now, I thought, and fight, shoot, shoot, shoot, and

they supposedly attacked with knives between their teeth, knives to gouge out your eyes and cut off your lips and your ears and your nose and your fingers and your genitals; we had to do something, we couldn't just hunker on our mattresses until they came and slaughtered us like docile cattle! The men bedded next to me came up and looked at the map. 'Man!' said Johann, an older telegraph worker to my right, 'Man,' he said and looked at the map and fell silent and stared at the map in silence, and my other comrades stared at the map too, and I held the map in my hand and had long since ceased to look and tried to reassure myself with the thought that the whole Moscow situation couldn't be that bad. Wasn't the fact that we were lying here idle the best proof that the lost battle had been just a trifle? Was it really so bad to be defeated once? Why, we'd beaten Poland, France, Norway, Denmark, Holland, Belgium, Yugoslavia, Greece, Africa, the world! But the major had gone running, and the colonel had held a speech: surely nothing like that had happened before? Or was it just proof that the Wehrmacht really was an army of the people? My comrades stared at the map. Suddenly it seemed like a betrayal to be sitting there openly displaying the map, this traitorous map, this enemy propaganda in disguise, and I muttered that I'd just wanted to see where Pearl Harbor was, where our brave Japanese comrades had destroyed the American fleet yesterday, and then I folded the map back up, eight times, and tucked it under the strip of canvas and put away the calendar I wrote my poems in, and after that I never wrote poems in that calendar and I never looked at that map again. At dinner we all got a mess-kit-lid full of rum; I downed it in one swig and finally I said to myself that the Führer would do it all right. He wasn't as dumb as Napoleon; Napoleon had marched into Moscow and then Moscow had burnt down and that had been the end for Napoleon, because then he didn't have any winter quarters; but the Führer hadn't marched into Moscow and Moscow hadn't burnt down, so it had to go on somehow, somehow, and General Winter wouldn't be in command forever and one day spring would come and then we'd advance victoriously once again, I thought, like a knife through butter, inexorably, in the spring. And in the spring we did advance again, I was sent to the air signal centre in Poltava as a teletypist and everything was completely back to normal: we were now in Poltava, I was a teletypist at a big exchange, the Wehrmacht sliced through Russia like a knife through butter, and its goal, which, once captured, would decide the war for good, was clear for all to see: Stalingrad!

The Battle of Stalingrad raged and the radio declared daily that it was a matter of days till the city on the Volga was conquered for good, but I didn't believe that Stalingrad would fall this winter; I predicted its fall in early summer. Not that I mistrusted our broadcasters; I simply knew better, it couldn't fall yet, this eastern war's see-saw rhythm was so clear! In the warm season, when the ground was dry and the farmland green, the front advanced hundreds of kilometres; in the muddy period the advance bogged down on mired roads, and finally in winter the front froze or shrank back dozens of kilometres, as the cold makes everything shrink, and dug in, only to thaw again in the spring and surge forward again in May, hundreds of kilometres into the vast eastern realm, until one day, maybe ten, maybe twenty, maybe a hundred years from now, we would stand on the Pacific, keepers of a new Alexandrian Empire. Following a night shift in the teletype exchange, I sighed and pulled wool socks over my foot wrappings and then put my boots back on; no, I didn't believe Stalingrad would fall this January or February. At thirty below you couldn't take a city, that was unrealistic; now our boys would dig in round Stalingrad, I thought, and then in April, maybe in May, Stalingrad would fall; in June assault boats would cross the Volga, in August the tank spearheads could reach the boundary between Europe and Asia at Uralsk or Orenburg, and I thought to myself that once the front had reached Uralsk or Orenburg we would be moved up to Stalingrad, as the signal centre of the Ukraine Air District Command always lay several hundred kilometres behind the front. At the moment we were in Poltava, in the heart of the Ukraine, and once the tank spearheads had reached Uralsk or Orenburg, we'd be moved up to Stalingrad, which of course would be called Tsaritsyn again then or maybe even Hitlerstadt, and it would be summer, verdant summer, and we'd breathe freer with the front advancing again. But now all that was still a dream, now it was winter, the storm howled outside, palm leaves of frost coated the windows, and though I'd just come from the night shift, I had to go outside to fix the defective cable to the freight depot.

I was a teletypist and normally wouldn't have had to go out fixing cables, especially not after a night shift, but several weeks ago an inspection commission had gone through the base and sent a good third of our signal unit and our telegraph construction squad to the front, so that those of us who were left behind had to do double duty while taking care of the outdoor jobs as well. Winding a scarf round my head, I thought morosely of the hours ahead: if I was lucky, the cable would have torn near the exchange, and I could finish in an hour and go to bed; if I was out of luck, I might have to walk the eight kilometres to the freight depot with my cable reel, and the whole morning would be shot; lunch, set aside for me by my comrades, would be cold by then, cold pease porridge or cold mashed potatoes with cold gravy, and if things were busy, and to all appearances they were, I'd be on duty again that afternoon! Goodbye, my lovely day off, when I'd planned to sleep in for once and then go to the soldiers' club! The storm yowled outside the window. Cursing, I strapped the safety harness round my chest.

Just as I was leaving the room, the telephone rang. I picked up the receiver and heard, to my surprise, the voice of Inspector Eichel, the mess officer who was filling in for the sick head of the work detail. Was it true that I was going trouble-shooting by myself, asked Inspector Eichel, and when I affirmed with some surprise, as Inspector Eichel otherwise took little interest in our welfare, he said that two Hiwis, Ukrainian volunteers, had arrived and we could use them from now on for unskilled jobs, and that he would send them over to me at once. I thanked him, he rang off, and I wondered, grinning to myself, what favour the natty Inspector would ask in return the next time I did night shift: a call to Bordeaux, where he ordered cognac for the staff from an acquaintance in the central commissary, or a connection with his wife in Dortmund. Probably Bordeaux, I thought; just yesterday I'd heard our office commander, Major Högner, chewing out the inspector because the mess was so dull and there was nothing decent left to drink. That was fine with me, Bordeaux was easier to reach than Dortmund. The door burst open, and a private from the orderly room came in.

'Are you the one who gets the Hiwis?' he asked.

I said I was.

'Get in here!' said the private and motioned with his hand. The two Hiwis stepped through the door.

I looked up, curious about the two lads. Despite my efforts, I'd had no contact with the civilian population so far: I never crossed paths with POWs; Lyubov, Tamara and Olga, the mess waitresses, blonde Valkyries with massive busts and behinds and wobbling cheeks from which their mouths blared cherry-red, were for the officers only and had nothing to do with lousy privates like me; the cleaning ladies and maids only shook their heads when we asked them something and said 'Nix Deutsch' and ran away so quickly that the filthy water slopped out of their buckets, and the town's inhabitants avoided us and gave us hostile looks when we passed, vanishing into their houses, and even through the curtained windows we felt their eyes like knives in our backs. But now I'd meet two true sons of Holy Mother Russia, and I imagined that two moustachioed Cossacks would enter the room, or two members of the God-Seekers' guild with blazing eyes and pale brows, white as lilies, but through the door, awkward, sheepish, each with a knotted bundle in his hands, came two lads my age with shocks of blond hair, healthy fellows with clean faces, broad shoulders and straight backs, and as soon as I saw them I thought that they must have German blood in their veins. Perhaps they were stray Volga Germans, perhaps even descendents of the House of Rurik, great-grandchildren of the Germanic migration the Russians had summoned to their land long ago to set up and govern a state for them, just like today. I held out my hand, and they took it shyly. The man who had brought them had already left.

'German you understand?' I said, purposely using broken German.

'Yes, sir, a little we understand and speak,' said one, the shorter of the two, and the other nodded.

'Are you from a German settlement?' I asked.

'No, sir, we learnt in school,' said the Hiwi.

'In a German school?' I asked in astonishment.

'No, sir, in Ukrainian school,' and the Hiwi said, now and then searching for a word, that from the fifth grade onwards their school had taught German as the first foreign language. I listened to him in disbelief, but then I recalled finding German books in some of the farmhouses where we'd been quartered: schoolbooks, readers, novels, poems, and I smiled and thought to myself that it was true, no nation could do without German culture, not even Bolshevik Russia, and I thought with satisfaction that under German rule Russia too would make something of itself again, a Bolshevik canker no more, no, a clean, orderly, civilized state, we'd pull it off all right, look at all we'd done already! The Hiwis stood inside the door twisting their bundles in their hands; I nodded at them benevolently and asked their names. The shorter one was called Nikolai, the other Vladimir, and I told them my name and said: 'Well then, to good fellowship!' and the two said: 'Yes, sir!' and I said: 'Enough of that, we'll use first names, of course!' Nikolai nodded happily; Vladimir looked uncomfortable. 'Put your things on my bed for now,' I said, and Nikolai and Vladimir carefully set their bundles on the blue plaid blanket covering my bed. Hopefully they don't have lice, I thought, alarmed, and almost moved the bundles to the floor, but then I left them where they were. Outside the storm blustered. I pointed to a cable reel. 'Let's go!' I said, and we went outside.

It had turned somewhat milder; the storm blustered, but instead of an icy howl its broad mouth breathed sea air and blew bellying clouds on ahead of it, cottony masses that warmed a little and raised hopes of snow, soft, white, warming snow with a clear sky above and the sun's mild orb, prophet of summer. Our HQ with its barracks lay outside the town at the foot of a clayey hill: ice bared its teeth all round, the sprawling land lay crusted with snow, the crust was cracked, piled up in scabby masses from whose jagged grey the blue-fenced town rose as though sprung up out of nowhere. Now, without the hill at our backs, the wind howled, and we walked quickly; in the town, which we had to cross, it might be milder. The clouds careened, a dog yelped anxiously. On the ice-covered roofs no smoke rose from the chimneys, only green domes loomed in the sky. The town seemed abandoned, no pedestrians on the streets, no lights in the shops, though the morning was still dim. Two muffled-up women stood in a gateway; when they saw us they vanished silently into the yard, closing the gate behind them. The wind had fallen, it was almost warm, not even twenty below. Of one accord we slowed our steps. A priest came striding from a side street; when they saw him the Hiwis bowed deeply, and the priest raised his pectoral cross in their direction, a heavy silver cross on which a broken man hung. Noise rang out from the soldier's club, and I thought to myself that after work, though it was frowned upon, I'd take the Hiwis to the soldier's club and give them a treat, cookies and tea, which was all there was.

To change sides on the reel, the Hiwis had stopped for a moment in front of a shop; bored, I gazed through the streaky window: broken bric-a-brac on tatty velvet, defective old-fashioned junk, battered sugar tongs for a hundred karbovantsi, for fifty a comb missing teeth, for two thousand a pair of shoes with holes, along with a wreath of paper flowers, scraps of cloth, a lacquer painting and a guitar whose bridge dangled from the strings. So that was the workers' paradise, and how must it have looked before we'd come along and brought a bit of culture and commerce, and freedom from the Bolshevik yoke! For we had come as liberators; here, as in every shop, hung a picture of the Führer, and the picture was captioned: GITLER OSVO-BODITEL', Hitler the liberator, and I thought with pride that once again it was us Germans saving Europe from the barbarism of the East, as we'd saved it before from the onslaughts of the Arabs,

Huns, Mongols and Turks, and I thought how splendid it was that all the peoples of Europe were united at last in the battle against their mortal enemy: Germans, Italians, Rumanians, Hungarians, Slovaks, Croats, the Flemish, the French, the Dutch, Luxembourgers, Spaniards, Montenegrins, Moors, Bulgarians, Arabs, Finns, Latvians, and far in the east the valiant Japanese, now joined by the Russian people's finest sons! I walked up to the Hiwis, who had moved on again, and asked where they came from, and Nikolai said they came from a village near Kharkov where their fathers had been farmers, the richest farmers in the village, and had fallen in the struggle against the commissars who forced their village into a kolkhoz.

What was a kolkhoz?

We trotted along; the Hiwis lugged the cable reel and I pondered what these kolkhozes actually were. I wasn't exactly sure; all I'd heard in school was that a kolkhoz was hell on earth for the farmers, and so I'd pictured a manor belonging to a commissar, that is, a rich Jew, with serfs who had been free farmers before the commissar stole their land, and Chekists to drive them onto his fields with the knout.

'Kolkhoz bad?' I asked.

'Kolkhoz bad, sir!' said Vladimir, and added something in vehement Ukrainian which I didn't understand, probably a curse.

'Kolkhoz bad, sir!' Nikolai repeated and spat. *'Chort s nime, yob tvoyu blegu mat'*!'*

'And now nix kolkhoz!' I said.

Nikolai shrugged. 'Nix kolkhoz, sir,' he said, and explained that the Bolsheviks had wanted to evacuate all the villagers, but he and his mother and his sister and Nikolai's people had hid until the Wehrmacht came.

'And now you're nix kolkhoz, you're farmers again?'

The two were silent.

A sleigh passed, jingling.

'Well, you'll get land soon enough, it'll all be sorted out,' I said quickly, and told them I'd look into the formalities needed to get their land back, and Nikolai said quietly: 'Thank you, sir!' Vladimir sighed and shook his head.

By now we had left the town; the field lay open all round, a sea of scabby ice with flocks of crows riding its waves. I looked up at the cable: as far as I could see, it hung from mast to mast unscathed; it seemed we'd have a long way to go. The cold climbed my ribs; the wind blustered; in the trees the ten hanged men swung stiff as clappers in the bells of the round linden crowns. Three days ago,

---

* Ukrainian: 'The hell with them, motherfuckers!'

returning from a trouble-shooting mission, I had
seen their hanging: they stood on upturned crates,
their clothing tattered, ropes round their necks,
and they clenched their fists and before plunging
to their deaths cried out words to the Ukrainians
whom guards had led out here to watch the execution as a warning against similar acts; a railway
track had been dynamited, and the ten were
hanged as hostages. They were ten farmers, and ten
unshaken voices had rung out before the fatal
plunge, and they'd hung here for three days now. I
shivered; the hanged men were shoeless. A truck
drove past, spraying up ice. The Hiwis shuffled
along the slippery road, necks tucked in, arms
pressed close to their bodies, planting their feet
heavily. I drew my shoulders up to my cheeks to
shelter my neck a little. Ice was forming on my scarf.
Ahead of us the road ran straight as an arrow; we
had to reach the freight depot soon, and the cable
still hung taut on the masts; no tear to be seen, no
visible defect, and I was thinking with dread that
the cable might not be torn at all, just frayed against
a mast somewhere so that the exposed wire was in
contact with the ground and I'd have to spend
hours looking for this contact point, when finally,
just outside the depot with its dully gleaming
tracks, I saw the damage: the cable was torn in the
middle between two masts, each half hanging slack
like the cord of a gigantic coachman's whip.

It was an easy type of damage to fix, and my task seemed simple: I had to trim both cables back to the mast and replace them with a new length of cable, normally just a few minutes' work. I strapped on the crampons and scrambled up the mast holding the end of the new cable between my teeth as it paid out from the reel; the dull spikes of the crampons found little purchase on the frozen wood; twice I slipped, caught by the safety harness, before finally reaching the top. Down below the Hiwis hopped round and waved their arms and rubbed their hands. I envied them: I couldn't manipulate the thin wires wearing the thick gloves, and when I worked with bare hands, the exposed metal stuck to my fingers. Finally my fingertips turned white and I had to come back down; the Hiwis kicked a crust of ice to bits with their boots and rubbed my hands with it, and then I climbed back up again. I have no idea how long the job took, but I know that when I climbed back down from the second mast, my eyes were stuck closed with ice. The wind swished over the fields. 'Let's go to the depot and warm up, it's just a few yards,' I said with freezing breath. The Hiwis nodded.

Of course the depot had no restaurant and no waiting room, but a few sheds stood on the ground between the tracks, and I hoped to find an orderly room somewhere with a glowing iron stove at which we could unthaw and store up a bit of warmth for the way back. The first shed we tried to enter was locked; a lieutenant stood in the door of the second; I saluted, and we headed the long way round the shed to enter by the back door, but as we turned the corner we faltered. Before us, backed up against the wall of the shed, stood mute ranks of people swaying gently at the hips. Ukrainian women and girls, standing three rows deep along the shed wall and swaying; they stood crowded together, arms linked, they stood and swayed gently like grass in the wind. Each had a bundle of things on the ground at her feet, a little bundle, clothing, a pot, a spoon, and they stood and the wind blew across the roof of the shed, and now we heard that they were not mute, humming softly, very softly, a crooning song. In front of the women stood guards in fur coats, rifles slung over their shoulders. A sergeant paced up and down, smoking; a locomotive shrieked, and a black freight train loomed up on the track.

We hadn't gone another step; I stared at the women, and one of the women near us turned her head and looked at me and looked at Nikolai and Vladimir, the two Hiwis with their HIWI armbands, and then she nudged the woman next to her and the line of women turned, head by head, and looked the Hiwis in the face and looked at their

HIWI armbands, and in silence, head by head, they turned away again. The Hiwis stood white as chalk, lips trembling. The freight train stopped chugging; grey smoke billowed out, a shroud of warmth; I hoped the Hiwis would run away under cover of this smoke cloud, but they stood where they were, frozen to the ground. The sliding doors of the boxcars rattled open, caverns gaped, in silence the women picked up their belongings and the sergeant yelled: 'Come on, come on, hurry up!', the soldiers pushed the women forward, and suddenly Vladimir cried out and dropped the cable reel and dashed towards the women, and one who had turned away turned back towards him and Vladimir cried out a name, a strangled cry. A guard leapt to intervene and shoved Vladimir in the chest and yelled at us to clear off; Vladimir clenched his fists; the guard reached for his rifle; I yanked Vladimir back and Vladimir, feeling my hand on his shoulder, slumped and turned and walked back round the shed, stumbling and hanging his head. Nikolai stood silently, jaws working. The women vanished in the darkness of the cars, and for the first time I saw what I'd seen a dozen times here at the freight depot, transmitted in countless teletypes: a labour transport was heading for Germany, for Berlin or Vienna or Essen and Hamburg, but now I saw: my god, they had no shoes on their feet, just bundles of rags, and paper from cement sacks tied about their chests and backs, and none of them had a blanket, and the cars were unheated, without the glow of a stove, straw lay thin on the floors, and ice hung from the window bars.

The sergeant stalked over. 'What are you gawping at?' he asked quietly. I reported and then Nikolai and I quickly picked up the cable reel. Vladimir stood in front of the depot, leaning against a tree; his eyes were closed, and he shuddered. I laid a hand on his shoulder and searched for words to say to him; I wanted to say that the women would surely be better off once they'd passed Kiev and that they'd be well taken care of in Germany, but I couldn't utter a word. I took out my cigarettes and gave one to each of them; we smoked and heard the chugging of the train, quickening as it faded, and then the locomotive whistled and the chugging dissolved into the grey day. Had she been his girl or his sister? I wanted to ask him, but I didn't. Now, with noon approaching, the road was busier; horse-drawn sleighs glided past jingling; the market women hawked their wares; singing rang out from the soldiers' club. We didn't go inside, and when I reported to Inspector Eichel back at headquarters, he said that the Hiwis would have to go straight back to work unloading provision crates, and as for me, said Inspector Eichel, clearing his throat awkwardly, unfortunately I'd have to help out in the afternoon shift too; the army command signal centre was out of commission, the underground cable destroyed, probably by partisans, so that all communications were now being routed via our teletype and telephone network. That was fine with me; I wanted something to keep me busy.

I wolfed down a few spoonfuls of cold pease porridge and asked my comrades on break to organize a double bed and a locker for the Hiwis, and then I went into the teletype room, sat down at my machine, took a packet of the telexes that lay round in tall stacks, got put through to Kiev and began to relay the messages. Regarded as an experienced and accurate teletypist, I always got the telexes full of numbers, code words and place names, and so I typed the situation reports that had come from the front labelled 'Vital War Information': 'Positions evacuated south of the Cherulenaya', I typed, and 'Failed breakthrough attempt near Oblinovskoye', and 'Forces withdrawn from Tatsinskaya', nothing but names and numbers in black block letters on a narrow white-grey strip of gummed paper that ticked along under the print: OBLINOVSKOYE, I wrote, and suddenly Inspector Eichel was standing behind me looking over my shoulder and saying, 'Good god, that's the situation at Stalingrad you're typing, I'll have to bring it straight to the boss, his youngest son's down there!' He snapped his fingers impatiently, and the moment I'd typed the last letter he tore the telex from the holder and hurried off to the boss.

I took a new packet, this time shipment reports; till now I'd always typed letter by letter, as I'd learnt, not registering the message of the text as a whole, but all at once I faltered; one of the reports, under Item 3 in the column 'Dispatched to the Reich', listed: 'Three hundred and twelve fem. labr. from Poltava for Hpt.lt.st.U' and then came Item 4: 'Cooking oil three tons for Wi.lei.U' and then Item 5: 'Calves 614 (six hundred and fourteen), cattle 530 (five hundred and thirty), swine 308 (three hundred and eight), all for Wi.lei.U, sgd. Sodelbring Chief Inspector', and I typed and saw the women standing in front of the shed, arms linked, swaying at the hips, softly humming ranks outside caverns of ice that rolled on wheels, and I heard Vladimir's cry and thought to myself that war was pretty damn tough and the lad had really taken it like a man, and then I relayed shipment reports from Krivoy Rog, the iron ore basin, that had to be passed on quickly to Berlin. I connected directly to Berlin and typed: 'Dispatched from Krivoy Rog to the Reich: iron ore twelve cars for DEGUSSA;* scrap metal fourteen cars for DEGUSSA; iron ore twenty-four cars for

* DEGUSSA: German chemical corporation; manufacturer of Zyklon B, a cyanide-based pesticide used in gas chambers.

DEMA; scrap metal eleven cars for DEMA', and I typed number after number and firm after firm and saw the trains roll by as I typed, the trains with the red iron ore and the rusty red scrap, and the old question that had tormented me even as a child rose up again within me: who does this wealth belong to, where is it rolling, who controls the economy, who sets the levers, does it all belong to the people, does it belong to Germany, or does it just line a few rich people's pockets like in the First World War or was that done away with or was that still so, I didn't know. I typed; it grew late; I typed mechanically, I was tired, the numbers on the strip of paper began to blur, the air had a musty taste. All I wanted to do was sleep.

As soon as the shift was over I went to my room. It was furnished as before, without a bed or locker for the Hiwis. I asked my comrades and learnt that they had already set up the bed and locker when the duty officer had come and begun ranting: what were they thinking, Germans and Russians in one room, that was simply impossible, the Russians were our slaves and that was that, however gladly they volunteered and lugged cable reels! I thought to myself what a raw deal that was and decided to intervene with Inspector Eichel first thing the next morning; today I was too tired, and there was no point anyway, the brass was all sitting in the casino, Inspector Eichel had had a pig slaughtered and my comrades reported that a shipment of red wine and cognac had come from France; I couldn't possibly disturb them now. And so I lay down and closed my eyes, but I couldn't sleep. I dozed, images came and passed before my eyes, an undecipherable flood of faces and wheels and branches and caves, drifting smoke, drifting snow, once I saw a hand very near. Then came a clown with powdered cheeks; he laughed and made faces and before him was a red blaze. The light faded and I sank through one more mist; now music seemed to be playing, then there was a rushing, and then I must have fallen asleep. But all of a sudden I started up: a strange voice rang out through the room; I had never heard it before, it was dark and filled the room like the pealing of alarm bells.

'Comrades, brothers!' said the voice, from above, from the room's loudspeaker. 'Comrades, brothers!' it said, and the words resounded like trumpet blasts. 'In Stalingrad, comrades, the Sixth Army is bleeding its life out in the ice and snow!' I lay paralysed, and heard with a dull thrill of matchless horror that it was a German voice that spoke to us, now questioning: 'For whom, comrades, are you sacrificing your life and happiness?' asked the voice, and we lay awake on our straw mattresses in the dark and heard the dreadful question, and each knew that the others were awake and listening, and no one got up to turn off the loudspeaker, no one, not I, not a soul, and this was enemy propaganda, one of the worst of crimes, and what we were doing was mutiny. It was mutiny: the enemy stood in our room, behind our lines, and we looked him in the face without striking him down, and I felt that the world had sunk away all round and there was nothing left but this room and this voice, and I heard this invisible German recite a poem:

Why, have you lost all sense of shame?

Let others perish if they're game.

But you can stop before you're sent

En masse to deaths you can prevent!

Come weaponless from out the trenches!

Who nee-

and then there was a click, and the voice broke off; the radio had been switched off at HQ.

No one said a word. We heard one another's breathing and the slightest noise of the straw-filled mattresses, and the worst thing was that no one cracked a joke. The breath caught, the silence hummed; I heard my heart beat and lay powerless under the brunt of the questions that gouged into my mind like shells into an open field: Sacrifices for what? Why the war? For Germany? Really for Germany? For who else?—and suddenly I felt a question rise in my mind as a flood rises: Do you even know what the others are fighting for?

Do you even know what Bolshevism is? Stupid question, I thought hastily, stupid question, what nonsense! and I saw the shop with the battered sugar tongs and heard Nikolai say: 'Chort kolkhoz!', but behind it suddenly I saw the farmers hanging from the gallows and the branches, the farmers and the farmers' wives and young girls and boys and old people too, and I saw them being led out to the green gallows with the sweet blossoms and the black branches with the crows and ice; ah, gallows, gallows, gallows, was that the trail we left across Russia's fields; and they'd all raised their heads as they walked to the gallows, and they'd clenched their fists, and with the rope round their necks they'd called out words a comrade had translated, meaning 'Long live the homeland!' and 'Stalin will triumph!' and 'Death to the occupiers!'. Was that how Untermenschen died? What gave them this strength, what goal were their eyes fixed on before they fixed forever? Why did they fight us when we were trying to liberate them from commissar and kolkhoz? It was a vortex, a maelstrom, every answer sucked away; suddenly I felt I knew nothing at all, not even why I was lying here in Russia and why my comrades were falling at Stalingrad and why there were Germans on the other side and what kind of Germans they were and what they were doing there: I knew nothing! The voice had long since fallen silent, and yet it remained in the room; it spoke its *why* loud and clear, and in this one silent minute, as each held his breath, I knew a question had sunk into my mind like a seed, no longer to be uprooted.

Then I fell asleep; I slept without dreaming; shots woke me. Thinking of the partisans, I jumped out of bed, but one of my comrades came in from the yard and said that one of the Hiwis tried to escape while being marched out and had been shot.

'Oh?' I said, trying to hide my agitation.

'Chest shot, dead on the spot,' said my comrade with a yawn and cut himself a slice of bread and spread it with syrup.

'Oh?' I said.

A dull dart dug into my heart.

'Cold today,' said my comrade, chewing, and then he went to the loudspeaker and turned it on, and we heard the Reich radio announcer: '... iron rampart, gripping the Volga, steadfast bulwark amid the onslaught of the Jewish-Asiatic hordes', and I stopped thinking that Stalingrad would fall early that summer, and outside the clouds were racing.

20 July 1944, The Attempt on Hitler's Life

It was eight in the evening, the sun in the west glowed blood-red on the shimmering marble, and Sergeant Major Buschmann and I were discussing 'The Embrace of Doom as the Central Core of the Germanic Worldview', the inaugural lecture in the German Department of the new Soldiers' College for whose first three-week course the two of us had been detached from the Athens Luftwaffe Exchange, when a courier arrived with orders from the duty station commander: we were to return to the exchange at once. Sergeant Major Buschmann objected that Captain Klapproth, our commander, had released us from all duties, even roll calls, for the three weeks of the Soldiers' College, but in vain; the courier repeated that his orders were to bring the two of us back to headquarters at once in his jeep. 'Nothing to be done, old man—that's the army for you,' Sergeant Major Buschmann said to me, rising to his feet, and since in following this order we had ceased to be academic equals of the same age and semester and were once again Wehrmacht soldiers of different ranks, he added: 'Get my bag from the cloakroom, Corporal!'

It would have seemed obvious, here in Athens, the city of noble torsi and temple ruins, to attend the lecture series on Greek tragedy from Aeschylus to Euripedes, but I was one of the few to choose the cycle 'Introduction to the Poetic Lore of the Edda, Focusing on the Völuspá', and there was a special reason for that. Even as a child I had written poems daily; they had always been dark, barely lit by hope or comfort, but ever since the lost Battle of Stalingrad I'd pictured nothing but apocalypses, where even the seas burnt and the howl of death rode the seething skies like massed clouds. Three of these poems had been published in a slender journal remote from literary circles, and obscure though the magazine was, they had found a reader who wrote to me and with whom I was soon exchanging friendly letters—my only correspondence, incidentally, except with my parents and my fiancée. This reader and friend, whose opinion I valued highly, had advised me to immerse myself in the Edda; there, he wrote, I would descry the deepest wisdom of the human race. When I received that letter, Kharkov had just fallen, and we were feverishly dismantling our exchange in Poltava to head for Kiev, and from there, now a cryptography specialist, I was transferred to Athens; I had long had no news from my unknown friend and had nearly forgotten his advice to read the Edda, but when I read the announcement of a lecture series on the Edda in the Soldiers' College's cleanly printed prospectus the recollection returned, and I quickly decided to attend the series. After reporting my decision I had spent several days worrying that Captain Klapproth might not release me after all, for we were overwhelmed; as the Wehrmacht's only exchange in the Southern Balkans that still had intact connections to the Reich, we had to relay the crucial army and navy reports as well, and there was a shortage, especially in the teletype exchange, of personnel even for the Luftwaffe's own needs. That was why I was worried, but the regiment's order was binding: two men, it requested, were to be released from duty for three weeks, and that's how I'd attended the inaugural lecture today with Sergeant Major Buschmann, and was now riding back to duty in the jeep, furious, paying no mind to the glowing crimson and green of the vineyards above the road.

I was furious at having to return, for the lecture had set me on fire; its thesis, that the highest racial and human type must bring on its doom together with its consummation, struck me as the most fascinating words of wisdom. And finally I had a copy of the Edda; I'd borrowed the heavy quarto volume from the College library and planned to do some reading that evening: on Muspilli, the gods' fiery end, and the Fenris Wolf who strained roaring at his fetters to tear the blond Aesirs' realm to pieces with his claws and fangs; I'd bought a pack of Macedonian cigarettes just for the occasion, and now I had to go back to the exchange, what a nuisance! I thought to myself that something out of the ordinary must have happened if we were being returned to duty despite being promised three weeks off; probably encrypted reports had come and were proving hard to decipher, perhaps there were just a few questions, but perhaps—and suddenly my heart stopped. Had it all been revealed? I glanced out the window: we were almost there, already driving through the lemon grove. The yellow fruit hung beneath dark leaves as though moulded from wax, creatures of the moon. Hanged men in the leaves; I shuddered. It can't be, it's simply not possible! I thought, but the question came back louder and louder: Why not? I felt myself go pale, as though both thought and blood were draining from my brain. The jeep was already turning into the pine forest whose palmy green hid our exchange. In two minutes we'd be there. Caught, then! I thought, and three black circles revolved before my eyes.

It can't be true! I thought.

For the past few months, though it was strictly forbidden, I had been sending and receiving private messages via the teletype network: one day, I believe it was in March '44, when the radio reported an especially severe air raid on Berlin, a

comrade whose family lived on Markusstrasse in
Berlin-Friedrichshain came to me, as I often com-
municated with the Berlin Luftwaffe Exchange, and
begged me to ask my Berlin partner whether
Markusstrasse 18 had been hit in the air raid. I
held back a long time before giving in, the harsh
punishment for such private enquiries having been
impressed upon me forcefully, but when I learnt the
next day that the building was unscathed, my
friend's cry of joy was ample reward for my fear!
Then an enquiry came from Berlin regarding the
fate of a soldier who had last written from Athens
and hadn't given a sign of life for six months; a
fixed, encrypted system was soon developed to
convey these messages, and it flashed through my
mind that this system had been exposed by some
mischance and now everyone involved would be
court-martialled and surely condemned to death.
That was the only thing it could be: we'd been
exposed, and the court martial awaited us! I saw the
packs of telexes, Vital War Information, as their
header indicated, the most urgent of all except for
the Führer's own telexes, often piling up for hours,
even days, on our desks because the lines to the
Reich were overwhelmed: enemy situation, supply
situation, partisan situation, gasoline situation,
truck situation, a red-exed stack of paper lurking on
my desk while I enquired in Hamburg whether
the last air raid had hit Hasselbroockstrasse 14 in

Eilbeck, my comrade Unger's home! I closed my eyes and saw myself standing before the court, the insignia ripped from my sleeves, my trousers belt-less and my shoes unlaced, and I heard the judge slam his fist down on the table and shout: 'Do you know what you've done, you swine? You stab-bed the Führer's war in the back, you went and sab-otaged his magnificent plans!' I choked on my answer, unable to make a sound, my tongue like a clod in my mouth.

The brakes screeched, the car stopped. Now! I thought, opening my eyes. Wires, masts, tents, plane trees; no armed guard. The sun glowed red on the dark agaves. I didn't breathe. A door opened with a bang; Lieutenant Fiedler, the head of the teletype office, came running towards us from the camouflage-painted barrack. Was he reaching for his gun? The air steamed round me, a seething wave washed my skin, then my mind cleared. The jeep was empty; ten minutes down the road and I'd be in partisan territory! All I saw was the lieutenant's holster. It was closed. Sergeant Major Buschmann stepped forward and made his report, which I didn't hear, and then I heard Lieutenant Fiedler say something about an extremely urgent job, and I breathed easy; I felt I was drifting from the ground and flying, I saw a red circle, dilating, bursting with a bang.

I remember nothing at all of the minutes that followed, though in the span of time it took to walk to the teletype office the lieutenant must have told me of the attempt on Hitler's life. Was I dismayed, was I outraged, was it my sense of deliverance from punishment and mortal fear that dominated? Or did I take the Führer's miraculous salvation as a matter of course, an elementary phenomenon like the sunrise that follows the darkest of nights? Probably the latter, but I no longer remember; those minutes are blotted out, my recollection resumes when I was sitting in the teletype office in the dust-whirling light of the low lamps and the lieutenant, tossing a pack of fresh texts marked with a red-boxed Vital War Information onto the desk, removed yesterday's enemy sitrep, which I had been about to relay to Berlin, from the machine and told me to drop everything else and first relay the messages he had tossed on the desk, all of them intended for the Führer's Headquarters. 'But the enemy sitrep has been waiting since yesterday,' I said in astonishment. 'Do as you're ordered,' said the lieutenant.

I shrugged. At the other end of the line my comrade in Berlin rang impatiently. 'Yes, yes, I'm coming,' I grumbled, and began transmitting the telex the lieutenant had brought me, but the longer I typed, the less I understood why it was so urgent to transmit these particular telexes. They were all so obvious! Without exception they were telexes from high-ranking officers, colonels and generals, commanders in Greece, Bulgaria, Albania, Yugoslavia and on the Aegean Islands, all assuring the Führer of their steadfast devotion and loyalty: '. . . prepared at all times, my führer, to execute blind and unquestioning every order you give . . .' wrote a major general; '. . . prepared, my führer, to follow you wherever you may command . . .' wrote a colonel; '. . . prepared as one man to joyfully lay down our lives for greater germany and for you, my führer, whom with unswerving loyalty . . .' wrote an air force general, and so the flood of assurances surged on telex after telex, and I didn't understand why this was Vital War Information and had to be transmitted to the Führer's Headquarters even before the enemy sitrep. Wasn't it obvious that the generals were loyal to the Führer, loyal unto death? The guard's telephone shrilled; the lieutenant hurried over. I saw his body stiffen as soon as he'd reported: evidently he was speaking with a higher-ranking officer.

'Yessir, Major', I heard the lieutenant say, and again: 'Yessir, Major', and then: 'I'm sure it's gone through already, Major, sir!' and right after that he said, 'I'll look into it at once, Major, sir!' Then he came over to me, hastily leafed through the telexes, placed one on top and hissed at me: 'Put that one through next!' Then he returned to the telephone and reported that the telex was being put through right now. I pricked up my ears, seeming to hear heated words from the receiver; the lieutenant stammered something and then, very clearly, I heard a voice from the receiver yelling that it was a scandal that a telex from a general of the infantry hadn't been put through immediately. All round the machines clattered. The voice broke off; the lieutenant hung up. I began typing again; the lieutenant paced nervously. '. . . congratulate you, my führer, in the name of all the officers and men of our division, on your miraculous deliverance from the plot by that infamous clique of jew-loving . . ' I typed, glancing at the signature, and again, I saw, it was signed by an aristocrat. They must have quite a guilty conscience, these officers and gentlemen, I thought, and all at once, as I mechanically finished typing, I realized what had actually happened. Criminals had thrown a bomb at the Führer, our Führer, the only man who could lead the Reich to victory through the abysses and maelstroms of war; a coterie of traitors had put its filthy hands round Germany's neck; I couldn't imagine how a German could even think of committing such an incredible crime!

Suddenly I heard harsh voices duel outside the door. I recognized the voice of our commander. 'Really, I beg of you!' I heard him say sharp and quiet, and: 'Strict orders, I'm afraid!' snarled an unfamiliar voice. I strained to hear; then the door flew open, and a lieutenant colonel burst into the clattering room so precipitously that his aiguillette slapped against his chest. Captain Klapproth followed, gesticulating desperately. The lieutenant reported to the captain; we eyed the intruder furtively. The captain asked who was transmitting the Vital War Information to the Wolf's Lair,* and the lieutenant named me. Captain Klapproth and the lieutenant colonel walked up to my desk. I went on typing as per regulations; to my own surprise, I was completely calm and not in the least disconcerted.

'When was the telex from Lieutenant General von Rossberg put through?' asked the captain.

The lieutenant looked at me beseechingly.

'It hasn't gone through yet, Captain, sir,' I said, still typing.

'Outrageous!' the lieutenant colonel bellowed, 'outrageous!' He looked over my shoulder. 'Why are you ignoring the telex from the Aegean Commander and putting through a piddling message from a divisional commander, a mere colonel?' the lieutenant colonel bellowed.

I typed.

---

*Wolf's Lair (Wolfsschanze): Führer's Headquarters located near Rastenburg, East Prussia (now Kętrzyn, Poland).

'Answer, man!' the lieutenant colonel bellowed.

The lieutenant stood as though paralysed. Anger seized me. I looked at the lieutenant for a moment, then went on typing. I was within my rights to keep typing; as he was not my immediate superior, the lieutenant colonel could not interrupt my work.

'I'll have the lot of you court-martialled!' bellowed the lieutenant colonel, and his hand twitched towards his pistol.

'Answer the Lieutenant Colonel!' Captain Klapproth said hollowly. I stopped typing and said that, as per regulations, I was transmitting telexes of equal status according to the date and time of their arrival. Then I sat down again and went on typing; I heard the lieutenant colonel bellow that he'd shoot me down on the spot, and I knew he wouldn't shoot, and suddenly I realized: they were scared, the whole bastard gang!

The bastards were scared, scared shitless, that was it, and these were the ones who'd never liked the Führer in the first place, this gang of posh *Vons & Zus*, the calcified aristocracy, the counts and barons who had a problem with the fact that in National Socialist Germany the people decided things and that officers and men ate the same food from the field kitchen and that our Führer was only a simple private who had a heart for his soldiers and knew ten times more about war than all those general staff shitheads! They had a problem with that, and so a crazy criminal had thrown a bomb at the Führer, and now they all came crawling and fawning up to the Führer again, and now each wanted to be the first to fawn up to him and pledge his loyalty anew. Bastards, I thought, typing more slowly, bone-headed, blue-blooded bastards, now you come crawling on your bellies again! and I thought about the face the lieutenant colonel would pull if the machine suddenly malfunctioned, the only connection to the Reich jammed, that could perfectly well happen, and I thought of how I could feign a malfunction at any time with an imperceptible motion of my hand. My fingers itched to perform this motion; that adjutant and his general were at my mercy, and if I didn't feel like working, well, they could see where that left them; my fingers itched, but I decided to leave it be.

Meanwhile Lieutenant Fiedler and Captain Klapproth were talking urgently to the lieutenant colonel; the captain held the general's telex with trembling fingers, ready to place it on my machine at a moment's notice; the lieutenant flipped through the stack of telexes to show the intruder that they were all meant to assure the Führer of the loyalty and devotion of his commanders in the Balkans, and the lieutenant colonel hissed that he didn't care, it was an unheard-of scandal not to prioritize a telex from the commander; he'd report the whole affair to the very highest authorities, and all of us, first and foremost this obstinate corporal, could brace ourselves for one hell of a court martial!

You won't report a thing, my dear man, not you! I thought and began typing the text Captain Klapproth had placed on my machine: '. . . ever ready to follow you, my führer, in unwavering loyalty and, filled with national socialist resolve, to smash all enemy plots . . .' I typed and thought how I'd never seen an officer as helpless and abject as the lieutenant colonel with his hand twitching for his gun, and as I thought it I almost laughed out loud. The lieutenant colonel made a note in his calendar and turned round and stalked out the door, followed by the captain. The lieutenant winked at me wordlessly, then followed the captain. Quickly I sorted the pack of telexes, putting the aristocrats' oaths of allegiance at the bottom, then went on typing. After a short while Lieutenant Fiedler came back and brought me a typewritten page with a red-boxed Vital War Information in the upper left-hand corner and told me to drop everything and transmit this message first. It was a report on the army lieutenant colonel's intrusion into our Luftwaffe headquarters, and it was addressed to the commander of Luftwaffe

Staff South in Vienna. The telephone shrilled, I typed the report and heard the lieutenant say, 'Yessir, General!' and 'Positive it's gone through, General, sir!' and the telephone shrilled all night.

All night long I typed declarations of loyalty; towards morning a comrade from the telegraph construction squad came and asked if I could put through an enquiry about his family in Breslau, he hadn't heard a thing for months and the mail was barely arriving now, and I said that that was impossible at the moment, now the bigwigs were using the telegraph. My comrade sighed; finally he went away; I really couldn't help him right now. At 7:00 hours my relief arrived, and I went off to sleep; at 13:00 hours I went on duty again. The declarations of loyalty had been transmitted; I was just about to put through the enemy sitrep from the day before yesterday when the alarm sounded, announcing a Führer telex. I put aside yesterday's enemy sitrep and picked up the Führer telex. It was addressed to all the Wehrmacht units and demanded immediate notification of the names of all generals, admirals, staff officers, captains, officers and naval officers who had relatives in enemy countries or any connections with foreign nobility or who had been members of a Freemasons' lodge, and these criteria were followed by a good dozen more suspicious indicators to be checked. We passed the telex on to

the respective headquarters; towards evening the
first reports came in, and my suspicion was con-
firmed: the many names transmitted in response
to the Führer telex included Lieutenant General
von Rossberg's; he was related to the Italian royal
family!

My relief arrived at 19:00 hours; I gave him the
enemy sitrep from the day before yesterday and
wished him a pleasant shift, and then I went to the
plywood shelter where I lived with eleven other
comrades and slipped in under the mosquito net-
ting. It was stifling in the shelter; at the table the
off-duty shift played skat and drank retsina. I
couldn't sleep; I tossed and turned on my cot, then
remembered that I had a copy of the Edda in
my knapsack. I took it out and opened it to the
Völuspa, the wise woman's vision of Muspilli, the
world's end, and it was as though I were reading an
account of our times:

> Brothers shall fight | and fell each other,
> And sisters' sons | shall kinship stain;
> Nor ever shall men | each other spare.
>
> Hard is it on earth, | with mighty
>   whoredom;
> Axe-time, sword-time, | shields are sundered,
> Wind-time, wolf-time, | ere the world falls
>   . . .

O'er the sea from the east | there sails a ship
With the people of Hel, | at the helm stands
    Loki . . .

The sun turns black, | earth sinks in the sea,
The hot stars down | from heaven are
    whirled;
Fierce grows the steam | and the life-feeding
    flame,
Till fire leaps high | about heaven itself.

Now Garm howls loud | before Gnipahellir,
The fetters will burst, | and the wolf run free
Much do I know, | and more can see
Of the fate of the gods, | the mighty in
    fight.*

I read no further; I shut the book and went outside, shaken. I smoked and watched the sun set behind the green agaves. Then I went back into the shelter and joined the skat game and was outrageously lucky too: I was dealt the three highest Jacks and declared Schneider, making five million drachmas apiece; in return I treated the others to a mess tin full of wine.

---

* Translation taken from Henry Adams Bellows' *The Poetic Edda* (New York: The American-Scandinavian Foundation, 1923), altered to reflect Fühmann's version.

The next day I asked Lieutenant Fiedler whether I could be granted leave to go back to the Soldiers' College and attend today's lecture on the Völuspa, but it was another five days before the sergeant and I were given leave again. On a radiant summer morning we rode into Athens on the bus; the Acropolis shimmered like snow against the blue sky, the hard green of its agaves broke from the slaty rock and in lofty majesty a vulture described a great circle above the sacred city. It was early in the morning, we passed one of the trucks that drove about the city in the mornings to collect the bodies of those who had starved to death that night and take them to Piraeus, where the light loads were bundled together and sunk in the sea. The bus honked; the truck swerved and we barrelled past, between vineyards where the sun already seethed in the grapes.

The sergeant major gazed ahead pensively, seeming to brood over a problem; I was meaning to ask him about it when he raised his head and spoke. 'A strange affair, old man,' he said, and added that he was about to tell me a story and, this was the strange thing, he wasn't sure if he had dreamt it or read it in the newspaper: it was said that the Führer, as he told the story now, had allowed the relatives of the 20 July conspirators to execute judgement upon the criminals themselves, stringing them on the gallows with their own hands to expiate the guilt of belonging to the clan of one so wicked, and he'd had a vivid picture, continued my classmate, of the son placing the rope round his guilty father's neck, tightening the noose and crying: I serve the Führer! and as my classmate said this it seemed to me I had heard something similar as well. I told him this and said that given Hitler's noble-mindedness it was quite possible that he had proposed this form of expiation, perhaps inspired by the Edda, and my classmate said that if I had heard it too, there must be truth in the story, for two dreams couldn't be so alike. I agreed; we had reached Athens, the city of the goddess of wisdom who sprang from Zeus' head; we drove through the crowds on Adolf-Hitler-Strasse; the sun shone bright, already singeing, and at the tables outside the cafes where the black-marketeers sat the waiters were unfurling the sun shades. Drumbeats: outside the royal palace Evzoni stood on guard in their white kilts embroidered with red and blue rings and their tasselled hats; the bus turned left, we got out, having reached our destination, an academy that now housed our Soldiers' College.

I charged up the stairs to the bulletin board where the day's lecture schedule was displayed, and read that the college had been closed for five days and was now continuing its programme, and under today's date in the German Department I found the announcement of the Völuspa lecture, overjoyed that I'd be able to attend after all, and I thought to myself that later on in the seminar I'd work out the contemporary relevance of this apocalypse along with the crucial distinction from the events of our days: Asgard would not fall, the Fenris Wolf would not devour Germany, for the attempt on the Führer's life, meant to usher in the Reich's destruction, had failed, the conspiracy was shattered and dismembered, head and limbs; the Führer lived and held Germany's fate in iron hands, and I knew that whatever the coming years and decades might bring, there was one unassailable certainty: Greater Germany's victory in this war!

On Sunday, 6 May 1945, I was still drinking coffee at my parents', wondering if I'd be able to stay home Monday as well. I decided to leave early the next morning after all: I had to report back from sick leave in Dresden on 9 May, and it was no stretch to reckon three days for such a journey. I flexed my right foot; it hardly hurt any more. I had been wounded in the foot during the retreat from the Balkans in the autumn of 1944, and following a ten-week rail journey was finally admitted to a military hospital near Oppeln; by then, as the dressing had been changed only twice during the journey, the wound was infected, a phlegmon had eaten inch-deep holes into my calf until the bare bone could be seen in the bloated purple-black flesh; the lower leg was supposed to be amputated, I had already agreed to it, and it would have been sawn off had not the Russian Vistula Offensive forced our hospital to evacuate and transfer its patients to Carlsbad, where I found a doctor who cured me without the scalpel. That was in the winter and spring of 1945; in late April, still hobbling,

I was released, and as the head physician was in love with my sister, who through a stroke of blind fate was working as a nurse at this very hospital, I had unexpectedly been granted ten days of sick leave, which I had spent with my parents; now they were at an end. Once again I ran through the stations between here and Dresden, but came to the same conclusion: I would have to leave early next morning.

I didn't want to think about that now. We sat round the table in the study, drinking coffee; throughout my leave, by tacit agreement, we hadn't spoken a word about the war, and we didn't speak a word about the war now either, but each of us felt that we could speak of nothing else. The canary in its cage splashed water from its bowl. My father cleared his throat; he looked at me questioningly, but lowered his eyes as soon as I glanced up at him. I had just been getting up the nerve to ask him how he saw the situation as an officer of the First World War, but now, as my father awkwardly cleared his throat and looked at me with questioning timidity, I suddenly felt that he expected me to answer the question, and I said offhandedly, as though stating the obvious, biting into a piece of crumb cake as I spoke: 'The miracle weapons!'

'Yes, the miracle weapons,' my father said, and repeated the word several times in a whisper to himself as was his wont; then he stood up abruptly, switched off the popular tune on the radio and went to the window. Mother buried her face in her hands and began to sob, finally running off into the kitchen. Through the open window, bellying the curtains, came the May breeze. There was a smell of cress and soil. The sky was blue. I joined my father at the window and gazed out silently. The hillside loomed lush brown and green, furrowed by snowmelt that rushed down to the valley, and where it met the clear blue sky two crags sprang like granite horns from its curved brow. The road was quiet, the houses snuggled in the sunshine.

'What a beautiful world it could be!' my father whispered, pressing his hands against the windowsill. The wood creaked. 'God's paradise!' he whispered, a heavy, thickset man, his hair gone silver. 'God's paradise!' he whispered and breathed the air in deep with its smell of tilled soil, and breathed it out as though tasting it for the last time, and, paying me no mind, went on softly speaking of the paradise this earth could be, and the hell it had always been, just because the world begrudged the Germans everything, even the free sunlight! A lark soared up. My father shook his head, then slammed down his fist, rattling the panes, and bellowed, a bull, but damping his bellow at once to a whisper: through what fault of Germany's had the world swept twice over its sacred soil with fire and sword, slander and conflagration, and in a barely audible whisper he answered his own question: all we wanted was the right to live, he whispered, a piece of homeland all our own, self-determination, that was all—and now? He broke off and gazed up to the sky, eyes moist, and I thought to myself that before the bitter end came the heavens must rend and God must appear to sweep the Red hordes into the ocean with one airy lift of his brow! The war lost—that just couldn't be! My father heaved a deep sigh and sat back down at the table. I poured coffee. Mother came back from the kitchen, eyes red, and helped me to another piece of cake.

'It's sure to work out with the miracle weapons, it's always worked out before,' I said confidently. 'But why don't they finally use them!' came my mother's anxious cry. I shrugged my shoulders. I didn't know either.

Then, as always when our family spent Sundays together, we played three rounds of parcheesi; we rolled the dice and moved the green, red and yellow cones along their circular path. I was green and had just captured a red piece about to reach home when I myself was knocked out of the game by Father's yellow piece, and yellow alone held the field. 'There you go!' Father said triumphantly, and suddenly he looked at the board and the piece he'd set down, and he slapped his forehead several times with all his might and cried, 'What a fool I am!' We stared at him; the canary peeped piteously. 'What a fool!' my father repeated, slapping his brow hard, 'What a fool, I must have been blind!' he cried, and said that everything had been right before his eyes and he hadn't seen it: We'd been mesmerized by the Russian advance like the rabbit by the snake's eyes, overlooking the fact that America stood behind us, ready to pounce on the Reds, and that *this* was Germany's big chance! I looked at the board with the yellow and green and red cones, and then I saw it too. The May wind soughed; I breathed deep. 'Do you really think?' Mother asked timidly, but Father jumped up and said excitedly that everything pointed in that direction: America's rapid advance in the west, the stubborn defence in the east, and Father said we were only waiting for the Americans and the Russians to slam into one another, and suddenly he slapped his forehead again and said he'd just realized why we hadn't used the miracle weapons long ago: we didn't want to needlessly destroy German territory; the Yankees would recapture it for us, that was the key to understanding the situation: they'd collide with a mighty crash, the Yankees and Russkis, they'd slam together so hard the sparks would fly, and then America with its men and its material and its bombs and its tanks would slice through Bolshevik Russia like a knife through butter, and all Europe would stand by America as once they'd stood by us, and he said that God couldn't have it otherwise, a Russian victory in this war would be tantamount to the destruction of good on earth. He stood massive at the table; his eyes shone. Outside the lark poured out its song. 'God willing!' my mother whispered. The sky was silky blue.

The next morning I took my leave and walked to the train station, which lay far outside town. It was a blustery May day; the föhn blew from the mountains, the meadows steamed, exhaling fragrance. At the end of town I was stopped by a patrol; its head, a familiar-seeming captain in ice-grey, stared flabbergasted at my leave pass and handed it without a word to his two companions, corporals in ice-grey, and the two corporals also stared at my leave pass as though at a chimera. 'Well, I'll be!' said the captain, eyeing me as though I'd just risen from the dead, and then he asked whether no military police patrol had checked my papers on the journey from Carlsbad, a journey straight through Field Marshall Schörner's command. I said truthfully that none had, and the captain shook his head and stared at the leave pass again and said I'd had the most incredible luck, showing this document to him, a friend of my father's; any other patrol would have strung me up on the nearest tree as a deserter! Dismayed, I protested that the leave pass was in order, and the captain said that was the crazy thing at a time like this when all leave had been strictly prohibited for months. Then he tore my paper into tiny pieces, buried them in the ditch with the heel of his boot, and wrote out a pass that said I had reported properly as a straggler and was taking the train to the next collecting point. 'Good god, man, make a run for it!' he said. I saluted and walked to the railway station, still limping slightly; I no longer recall what happened then, only that contrary to my expectations the train was not the least overfilled and I even got a seat on the window, and the train wheels clattered, the same beat over and over, and the telegraph wires swooped up and down. Then the train stopped between stations; we were told that the tracks were cut and we'd have to march ten kilometres. The travellers, almost all of them soldiers, left the train. I looked round for a familiar face, but there was no one there I knew; most of the men falling into some semblance of a march formation were older, with sullen faces. There were several Hungarians as well, short, lean men with khaki uniforms, carrying tied-up bundles in their hands, poor devils, one with shoes full of holes, another with a tattered coat. We jogged along, to my right a lance corporal from the engineers, to my left an infantry platoon sergeant; in front of me I saw the faded ultramarine of the sailors and the clay-brown of the labour conscripts and the black of the tank drivers and the grey-brown of Organization Todt* and the green of the military police and the grey-green-red-brown mottled camouflage suits made of tarps and the dirty white of canvas with the *Volkssturm*** armband, and I realized with surprise that this motley crew was now the Wehrmacht. We jogged along like this for an hour; then we came to a small town and turned onto a square. The square was abandoned, not even a cart stood outside the shops and arcades; beyond the square, black on two pillars, I saw a railway overpass loom against the sky like a guillotine blade in its frame, when suddenly, without a sound, a huge flag fell down fronting a facade, not a swastika flag, its colours blue, white and red, what was that? The flag unfurled and with it came a roar; past the square people swarmed together, we heard shouts and footsteps resound; three men were running over the tracks and threw themselves down and suddenly there was a machine gun up there and hot granite sprayed on the marketplace. I dodged behind the nearest arcade pillar and threw myself to the ground, then grabbed my

---

* Organization Todt: Named after its founder Fritz Todt, the organization was responsible for most major civil and military engineering projects in the Third Reich.

** *Volkssturm*: German national militia founded as a desperate defensive measure in late 1944, conscripting men aged 16 to 60.

rifle from my back and chambered a round and shot at the machine gun, but already tanks rolled across the square, the railway crossing flew apart, a rip went through the facade with the flag. An inhuman cry broke through the roaring and rat-a-tat-tat; a salvo swept the colonnade, and suddenly a man stood before me, tall, black, in shoes, not in boots, yelling: 'Down there, cover the bridge!' I jumped up from cover and ran towards the bridge, beside me a sailor and someone else who suddenly fell over, and then we reached the bridge and threw ourselves down, but the bridge was deserted. The stream it crossed shot along swirling, torn branches rode the grey water. I heard artillery fire and machine gun salvoes; the noise receded, a worker's cap drifted on the water. I looked up at the square—clouds of dust whirled over rubble, the Czech flag hung in tatters: so that had been the uprising, they'd tried to stab us in the back, but once again we'd emerged victorious, and I saw how the flag hung in shreds. We stood there for a while, the noise ebbed, and then someone took us over and assigned us to something that called itself a flak shock troop.

And I recall a bare room where we, the new arrivals, hunkered till evening, forbidden to leave. Double sentries with machine guns stood at the gate, now and then Gestapo officers crossed the yard, and suddenly word went about that last night one of the platoons in the flak shock troop had killed their lieutenant and deserted. I took in the rumour like one of those legends too improbable to be untrue. Why shouldn't it have taken place, when unheard-of things were happening, revolts, mutinies, murders, and the unheard-of nearby as well: the Americans had supposedly already shot at a Siberian infantry regiment, one reported, and a second said that the Americans had already occupied Prague and were approaching our position in forced marches, and a third was convinced that we'd be fighting side by side with the Americans in just a few hours' time, because the Americans wouldn't give up Bohemia and Moravia now, they'd stipulated that as their price for the second front! One man asked where we were, anyway, and I got out my pocket calendar with the map of the world, but it didn't do us any good; Bohemia was just a dot, no larger than a pinhead. Evening fell; there was potato soup, and we ate in the dark; the power plant, it seemed, had been blown up by the insurgents; we hunkered in the grey of dusk and thought about the Americans and seemed to hear an artillery battle very far away, when a corporal came in and ordered us to go with him; a brass hat from the High Command was here and wanted to speak to us. We nudged one another: surely he would bring us the news that we had allied ourselves with the Americans.

We groped our way down dark corridors and finally entered a large, empty room where two tallow lamps burnt. We lined up, more platoons crowding in behind us, we stood cheek by jowl, cobblestones that breathed, and then a door was flung open and someone yelled 'Attention!' Standing far to the back, I saw nothing and only heard a raspy voice report and an oily voice say thank you and that now Colonel Pauli from the High Command would speak to us. A shapeless, bloated head rose above the front rows: the colonel must have climbed onto a footstool. His eyes sized us up, I saw the flickering shadow of his skull on the wall like the image of a mammoth skull in a primaeval hunters' cave, and the colonel began to speak, softly, in a halting voice; sometimes it was almost a whisper, but what he said in that muted voice made a thrill run through us: it was nothing less than our imminent victory! In the next few days, perhaps hours, the war would be decided, the colonel said, and his shadow flickered on the chalky wall; the fateful turn was at hand, said the colonel, and slowly, very slowly he pronounced those words: 'The miracle weapons!'

So it was true! It was silent in the vault, shadows loomed on the wall, it was deathly silent, and I saw them fall from the sky, the miracle weapons, the magic bombs, St Michael's wrath! The colonel was speaking quickly now; he gave us his officer's word of honour, he said that he'd seen the miracle weapons with his own eyes, and his heart had stood still when their devastating effect was described, and he lowered his voice and whispered that the miracle weapons would destroy all life within a hundred kilometres and that the leadership would use them the very next day, but before that, he said, we had one last combat mission to complete: some of our comrades were still stuck in a pocket on the Moravian border, we'd have to rescue them so they wouldn't be wiped out tomorrow when our leadership deployed the miracle weapons, and the little flames wove in their bowls of tallow. 'Our victory is inevitable, comrades!' cried the colonel, and suddenly he jerked up his hand and yelled '*Sieg Heil*, comrades!' and we cried '*Sieg Heil*' three times and the vault resounded.

Then we were groping our way down the dark corridor to the yard where the trucks waited. We climbed in, it was crowded, we were almost sitting on one another's laps. We smoked the last of our cigarettes, no one spoke, outside the night slipped past with its smell of cherry blossoms and ferns; it was a clear starry night and we smoked and looked at the stars and no one said a word. We drove quickly, the wind whistling round us. I had managed to get a seat in the front left corner, where one could lean back; it was more comfortable than in the middle, cold, but that didn't bother me. The stars blazed; I sat squeezed in the corner on my knapsack and smoked one last cigarette and thought of how the world would tremble tomorrow when the miracle weapon did its work, and the truck slowed down, the vehicles crowded together, truck upon truck, here and there tanks, jeeps and motorcycles; until now everything had rolled southward, but now, first a trickle, then a stream, then a river, traffic came in the other direction, northward; truck jostling truck and curse jostling curse, the columns slowed, we drove at a walk. We drove like that for about an hour; once someone shouted from one of the trucks heading north: 'Where on earth are you going?' and I shouted back: 'To Moravia', but the truck had already passed. It was a bright night, I saw the apple trees on the roadside, and the lindens, gentle hills rose on the horizon, gentle rolling hills, and mist billowed white on the meadows. It was a velvet night; I breathed deep, and suddenly everything seemed utterly unreal, Nirvana, a velvet dreamland, reality no longer. Men shouted from the oncoming vehicles; already nodding off, I couldn't understand what they were shouting.

Then someone shook my shoulder and I lurched awake; with a stale taste in my mouth, I saw wearily that we had stopped on some forest road.

It was late at night, the men snored, but my neighbour, a thirty-year-old private, was awake. It was he who had woken me, and he held his finger to his lips as I started up and motioned me to listen. Outside the truck voices whispered excitedly. 'There's no point any more!' one voice said, and 'How do you know it isn't all just enemy propaganda?' said the second. I peered through a crack in the side of the truck. It was two cavalry captains: they walked down the long column, smoking and whispering. 'Who on earth is supposed to be in command now?' asked the first. I listened intently for the answer, but the answer could no longer be heard. 'They want to sell us, man!' said the private. Astonished, I asked why, and the private said I shouldn't play dumb, I knew just as well as he that the war was over and our officers were just sending us to be slaughtered by the Russians so that they could escape scot-free to the Yankees. Suddenly I understood the shouts from the trucks heading north, and shock seized and shook me as a cat shakes a mouse. The private had leapt to his feet. The officers were out of sight. I stared into the forest: the spruces at the edge loomed grey, darkness yawned behind them, and yet it was a bright night. All at once I thought of the lads who had killed their lieutenant and run off into the woods, and thought suddenly that they were free, free men in the Bohemian woods with their thickets and clefts and ravines, and I felt something menacing approach with giant steps: the hour when I myself must decide what to do.

A deer dashed across the road.

My heart pounded loudly. The hour had come.

'What should we do?' I whispered. 'Whatever we do, let's stick together; when the officers are gone, we'll drive off,' the private said. I nodded. The cavalry captains came back. 'Turn round!' one of the cavalry captains shouted to the driver. The motors started; the trucks charged out of the forest. The sleepers woke with a start. 'What's going on?' one asked, rubbing his eyes. 'We're going home to Mother, Grandpa!' said my friend.

The trucks drove back; dawn broke. Voices buzzed; I heard them all without hearing them. We passed through a town where people swarmed about something burning in the marketplace; I stood up to get a better look and saw sacks that popped and hissed like powder as they burnt. Several young soldiers stirred the crackling fire with long sticks, and now and then one hurled in a bottle that immediately jetted flame. 'The idiots are burning the flour!' the private yelled. 'Should the Russians eat it?' asked the man in front of me, a sixty-year-old militia private. 'And we should eat dirt?' I screamed wildly. Then the people cried out and scattered and blue fire crept between their feet; fiery blue rivulets spilt across the market-place, in one desperate spurt our truck put the marketplace behind us.

We drove a while longer, then reached the main road that led west, and a slow flood of vehicles filled it as a river in spate fills its bed, wedged and locked together, radiator to exhaust pipe and front wheels to back tires. From everywhere they flooded westward, trucks, tanks, scout cars, jeeps, buses and motorcycles, all the Wehrmacht's vehicles flooded westward, the road was clogged with rolling vehicles, how could even a motorcycle squeeze in! Throngs of soldiers ran across the open field. A bazooka lay in the ditch by the road. 'Officers to the front!' yelled a sergeant. No officers came. 'They've bailed out!' cried a shrill voice. The trucks began to seethe; suddenly horror filled me. The trucks spilt over, brimming with twisted faces and screaming voices; I barely managed to grab my rifle and knapsack when the flood lifted me from the truck and carried me to the main road amid the panting herd.

I let myself be carried; a hand seized my arm. It was my friend. 'Do you have anything special, cigarettes or chocolate or something like that?' he yelled in my ear. 'Brandy,' I said, understanding. We elbowed our way through the milling crowd and ran up the shoulder of the main road a bit, then jumped onto the running board of a tarp-covered truck. 'Get down or I'll shoot!' yelled the driver, but I had already screwed open my canteen and held it under his nose. The driver sniffed; then he asked 'Full?' and I said 'Full,' and closed the canteen and shook it, and the liquid barely sloshed. 'Hurry, crawl in!' said the driver and tucked the canteen under his shirt; 'Hurry up!' he said, 'and don't let anyone see you, there's baggage from the Army staff in there!' 'And you take stuff from poor folks like us?' the private asked indignantly. The driver waved his hand irritably. 'Not what you think, just pictures and stuff!' he said.

We crawled under the tarp and huddled on lead-sealed crates. It was dark, with only a ray of light falling through a grommet. The truck jolted along. We had been moving for several minutes when we felt a violent impact; the truck stopped, we rolled against the tarp, wood splintered on iron, cries rang out, shots cracked; I flung open the tarp and saw that we were in the woods again and had run into the truck in front of us; the cabin door was open, the driver had vanished, all round the men were jumping from the trucks and running into the woods. I saw it even as a dust-crusted motorcycle stopped by our truck; the driver, in an earth-brown uniform, with red on his cap, jumped off and waved his submachine gun and yelled: 'War kaput, kamrad, no gun, voina kaput!' and I heard it like the voice of the Infernal Judge and jumped from the truck and ran past the Russian's reaching arms on into the forest, and in this instant I was completely sure that it was all just a dream. It was all just a dream: I was running in a dream now, I was always running in my dreams, always through a dark spruce forest, and now I was running through a dark spruce forest, and the boughs and needles slashed my face and I felt nothing, not a thing, it was just a dream, I was lying in bed and had to go to school and soon the alarm clock would ring, five more minutes, then I'd fall out of this nightmare and wake up in the sunshine and everything would be as it used to, the pear tree blooming outside the window, the clouds drifting in the sky, no more battle and hubbub, no more war and strife, it's blissful peacetime, and there came a ring, the alarm clock rang, *rrrrr* it rang, I heard it ring, it cracked into my dream, my forehead hurt, phantoms ran past, phantom cries, I stood with a torn-off bough at my feet and felt for the bump on my forehead and saw that my hand was bloody. Keep going, just keep going, this wasn't a dream, now artillery boomed behind us; keep going, just keep going, just get away from the Russians! I ran, and the woods thinned out; I ran more slowly, all round the phantoms scattered, my face burnt as if I'd fallen into a thornbush, the artillery shrieked.

Suddenly I was alone. I ran, my lungs gasping, I ran, keep going, just keep going, I don't know how long I ran, I no longer felt my body, and suddenly my foot slipped, something glittered on the path, I slid, the glitter was metal, I fell and lay on a pile of the gorgets the military police wore to identify themselves. The gorgets clinked; I wallowed in the gorgets like King Midas in red gold and I was more than he! The gorgets of the military police, and those who had worn them had been like gods, I thought, and now the godlike symbol was shed, glittering gorgets, rubbish now, scabs from pox, and their former wearers blundered through the woods now and no metal clinked on their chests, they made no arrests now, they strung no one up on the nearest tree, now they were naked themselves and fled through the woods, hunted dogs, and look, the trappings of rank lay there too, epaulettes and stars, a captain, look there, a major, a colonel, now all of them were just like me, I was no soldier now, now I was free, and suddenly I couldn't help laughing, I lay in the pile of gorgets holding a colonel's epaulette in my hand and laughing like a madman and artillery fire boomed all round, in front of me and behind me artillery fire boomed; bullets slapped down, and all at once the thumb-thick branch of the spruce before me fell severed to the ground. My laughter broke off; I saw a ditch and rolled into it, and as I lay in the ditch on the soft moss I felt unable to take another step, and then I realized I'd left my rifle and knapsack in the truck. The knapsack, that wasn't so bad, but the rifle! What would I do now if the Russians came? Suddenly in the blur of needles I saw the hanged farmers with their feet of ice, and I scrambled up again and ran through the woods. And then the woods came to an end; I saw an open field, soldiers standing with their hands up: prisoners! I threw myself down and saw my comrades slowly lower their hands and sit down on the field, and then I saw a Russian in a long earth-brown coat with a bayonet gleaming on his rifle. The shadow of the spruces fell on the open field; I had run westward, in the right direction, but the Russians were in the west already too, the path to freedom wedged shut!

So that's how it ends! I thought, like a beast on the field! In the forest shots rang out; the Russians must be combing the forest; they had an iron comb and ran it through the forest, and I was a louse it caught. I took my pocket knife out of my trousers and opened it; the blade flashed, how badly would it hurt? I was a louse, but they wouldn't catch me alive! I ran my nail along the edge and scratched at it a bit. The edge was dull. I stared at the blade: a grey piece of steel with rust spots on it, round rust spots, that would be torture, nothing more! The prisoners on the field lit a fire. And what if the Russians were nothing like that? What if they let us live? If they brought us freedom? Nonsense, that was all just cheap camouflage: shots whipped past, that was the reality! I struggled to my feet; if I was going to die, let me at least take an honourable bullet! I staggered down the forest aisle, and someone called softly: 'Hey!' I whirled round, scared to death; the aisle was empty. Again came the soft call: 'Hey!'; it came from a bramble patch, and I recognized the private's voice. I crawled up to the bramble bush; it seemed impenetrable, a tangle of wiry snares and sharp thorns. I crawled, shredding skin and uniform, but then a den opened up. 'No one will find us here!' said the private. His face was horribly scratched, his hands and neck bloody. I gasped that the Russians were already west of the forest, and the private nodded mutely. I looked him in the scratched face, and in my heart a tiny spark of hope revived: at least I wasn't alone now. 'Chin up!' said my friend, 'As long as we're still fucking round, all is not lost,' and then, in a whisper, he laid out his plan to me. We'd hide out in the daytime and only march at night, he said; the Americans were forty kilometres off, it would be a fluke if we didn't make it, even if we had to crawl on our bellies all night like snakes.

'And then?' I asked faintly.

The private whistled through his teeth. 'Germany's fucked, you can write it off for the next thousand years,' he said. The air in the den was green. 'And?' I whispered feverishly. 'The world is wide,' said the private and pulled out his cigarette case; he took a cigarette in his fingers, turned it this way and that and finally put it between his lips, but didn't light it. 'The world is wide, and Germany's fucked,' he said, sucking at the cold cigarette, and he said he'd go to the Foreign Legion or the English colonial troops, German Landsers would soon be in great demand, he said, the best-trained soldiers in the world and the only ones who knew the East, and he said he'd been on board since thirty-six, and he recited: Austria, the Sudetenland, Poland, France, Yugoslavia, the East, Italy, his tenth year now, and I wondered why he was just a private. He'd wanted to study once, philosophy and history, said the private, but now he didn't give a damn, he was a soldier of fortune now, and a soldier he'd remain!

The shots had faded, but a new commotion arose: a troop of soldiers ran panting past our den, down to the edge of the forest, only to race back again. I thought of what must be happening to our comrades on the meadow: surely they were being taken away troop by troop and killed somewhere in the forest, the forest was large! 'Germany's fucked!' said the private and took his boots off and tucked them under his head, and then he said dreamily: 'And yet—years lived like gods, I don't regret it!' and he conjured up life in this war once again: how the masters walked the earth, its peoples before them, caps doffed, bowed to the ground; years lived like gods, pharaoh-like upon the backs of the slaves, seeing the whites of the enemy's eyes and knifing him in the gut and taking his women and laying them down, hands on their throats, and drinking champagne in Paris and Bordeaux where the brothels had mirrors for floors, oh, days lived like gods, no regrets at all! I listened to him breathlessly and realized all at once that the war was over now and my friend had taken it as the gambler takes the roll of the dice, and I thought that now Germany really was fucked; they'd turn it into a potato field, that's what they'd decided in Yalta: potato fields, the women off to the brothels, the men off to the Siberian lead works, and I thought of how tourists from round the globe would wander Germany's razed cities and officious guides would cry: 'Ladies and gentlemen, here you see the biggest ruins in the world, the Cologne Cathedral and the Palace of Aachen . . .' and then it occurred to me that aside from Breslau and Oppeln I knew nothing of Germany, neither the Palace nor Cologne nor the Moselle nor the Rhine all I'd ever wanted was to go home to the Reich, and now the Reich was fucked, and actually this was none of my concern, I thought, I didn't even live in Germany, I was Czechoslovakian, I'd always been Czechoslovakian, none of this was my concern, it was all just a misunderstanding, and I thought to myself that I didn't have to go to the Foreign Legion, I could go home, the war was over, I didn't belong to Germany, no one could do a thing to me! But then I thought to myself that the Russians didn't respect international law and wouldn't distinguish between the Reich Germans who had begun the war and us, who had just gone along with it, and I thought that first of all I had to get to the Americans forty kilometres from here, forty kilometres off, a night march, no more, the last march in this war. The private wrapped himself in his blanket; we lay in a bramble den, Germany was fucked, soldiers stumbled through the forest, shots still echoed, and maybe they really were shooting at one another, the Americans and Russians, and it wasn't the last day of World War II, it was the first day of World War III already, and Germany, my sacred Germany, would conquer the world after all!

When the leaders of America, England and the Soviet Union met in Potsdam to deliberate on Germany's post-war fate, I was unaware of it, and even if I had known, it probably wouldn't have interested me: Germany was conquered; now it would be destroyed, we were headed for a life in bondage, and I had accepted this fate. I hadn't managed to break through to the Americans; for three nights we had stolen through the woods, westward and southward and finally to the north; on the third day the military police under General Schörner, who had ordered the soldiers to fight on, hanged my friend the private on a maple tree for desertion; I had to watch helplessly from a distant hill—we had gone exploring on two diverging paths—and soon after that I was seized by a Russian patrol and swallowed by one of the processions of thousands trudging eastward, and I had trudged eastward, eastward, towards the east, wondering if a quick death at the end of a rope mightn't have delivered me from the horrors of captivity that awaited us, and I trudged eastward and slowly the questions died away, and now I no longer thought a thing. The water glittered blue; shadows leapt in the distance, were those dolphins? I saw it, and looked no closer. I lay with my comrades on deck thinking nothing and hearing the waltzes from the foremast; the waltzes played incessantly: *The Blue Danube* and *Vienna, City of My Dreams* and *Is That You, O Smiling Bliss?* and I heard the blaring voices of the singers, the same places always broken by scratches, just as I heard the lapping of the waves, no longer wondering whether the captain played the Viennese waltzes to give us a treat or to torment us by evoking the sounds of times past. I thought nothing; I dozed, half-asleep; we'd spent over five weeks huddled in a freight train, forty-four men in one car, rolling southeast, and now we lay on the deck of the ship, drugged by the sea air and the mild sun and the sweet sense of satiety. On the train journey I'd been perpetually hungry, but now I was full, I'd eaten bread and fish, a third of a loaf of bread and a big piece of dried fish and ten cubes of sugar; we'd been told these supplies would have to last until we reached the camp, but I hadn't cared and neither had the others; I stretched myself out and ate bread and fish and sugar and drank water and breathed sea air and now I was full and half-drugged and the ship sailed over the Black Sea. 'Waltzing, oh waltzing in dreams!' a woman's voice blared from the foremast. The sky shone in the purest of blues. Far off, from the sea, leapt glittering shadows.

We sailed two days and nights like this, I believe; I can't say exactly, as I spent the time drowsing. I no longer know the ship's name and what the captain looked like and how we came on board; all I know is that once we boarded the captain and the station commander had an argument, evidently as to whether we should be housed on deck or below deck, and then I know we stretched out on the planks of the deck and ate all our provisions, and then the waltzes played and the world grew dark between sea and sky, and the next thing I remember is that land was drawing near.

I seem to recall that someone shouted 'Land!' and that I heard it and lay where I was, and I don't know if I saw the land drifting towards us, looming past the bounds of my gaze; I know only that its image filled my eyes all at once as a flash flood fills a narrow valley: brown-green beneath a glass-bright sky, the mountain arched, a giant's knee, the city rising towards it up the slope like dirty snow. The white of its houses was filled with holes, gleaming dully in the midday sun, crumbled remnants of a fairy tale on the brown mountain slope, and from the blue water loomed a red skeleton. The skeleton was made of iron, a gate plunged in the sea, long and flattened like a prised-open clamp, sharp as fishbones four rods rose from its flank, and the ripped stern of a ship half-filled it. Our steamship moved dead slow, since the harbour was littered with wreckage; beyond the ripped stern chunks of concrete lay like giant pebbles, behind that a mast impaled an airplane fuselage, and from the city the stink of cold smoke drifted through the strains of the waltzes. I was on my feet, staring aghast at the city and the harbour. The water had turned brackish, with iridescent slicks of oil. Without breathing or saying a word we stood and stared at the city, a crushed seashell above the beach on the mountainside. We stared at the city and waltzes played: *Vienna, City of My Dreams*; I was sitting in Café Sacher and saw a face flicker in the mirror's crystal; the mirror shattered and the city lay in shards and I stared at it and said: 'My god!' Suddenly someone laughed, but I heard it as if from afar; now the ship had halted, vibrating; masts bristled all round, the buildings on the harbour were sliced open on a slant from roof ridge to foot, and I thought with a shiver that the war had done all this: war had passed over the earth, the big black charburner with his beard and his rod, and he had laid about him with his rod, laying into harbour and city, and now the ships lay wrecked and the cities ravaged, that was the war, War the Charburner with his iron rod, sent by a god; what was a mere man in his sight? Suddenly I felt a dull hunger. The ship had glided to the rubble-strewn pier; we disembarked, and as we lined up a rumour arose: each convoy, the word went, would be assigned to a city which had been destroyed and which it would have to rebuild, and our city was Novorossiysk, which lay here before us, and when we had built it back up again we would all be released. The rumour leapt through our ranks like sound through the air; I heard it buzz in my ear and stared at the city and thought in despair: We'll never pull it off! We stood on the pier and stared at the city and my gaze climbed from building to building: I saw beams dangling from iron girders and stripped stairs and walls with holes like mouths and floors gaping open; I saw bricks heaped on bricks and thought helplessly how long it would take to cart off just one of the rubble heaps and dump it into the sea, much less rebuild the city, house by house and street by street and district by district—a whole nation couldn't pull it off, and we were just one ship's convoy! I saw the city and the rubble and thought I'd spend my life here toiling in the rubble, a carter in the rubble of Novorossiysk, chained to the cart like a prisoner to the galley, and suddenly I thought: It's only fair! The thought lasted a mere second and I forgot it again at once; it flashed like lightning through the night of my mind, the darkness swept back in after it, and only months later, with great effort, did I recall it. It's only fair! I thought, and already I'd forgotten; my stomach growled; we stumbled ashore; all round in the streets the rubble was shovelled to the sides, the burnt walls stank, we shuffled along. I hung my head, not wanting to see the shattered walls; the war had laid about blindly with its charburner's rod, and I wondered how long it takes to build the wall of a house: a day, a week, a month, I didn't know. We shuffled along; suddenly an old woman was standing at the rubble's edge looking at us and I lowered my gaze and looked at the heels of the man in front of me, two boots shuffling forward, one torn, the leather peeling, and suddenly I thought they'd come out of the ruins now and fall upon us and kill us, those who had survived, the victors now housed beneath the stones; I raised my head and saw the waste of rubble, the singed white facades, half a bathtub stuck in a window, and then I saw shuffling heels, nothing more. We walked through the city, we must have walked that way for an hour. People appeared as though from invisible fog; they looked at us and said nothing and we shuffled mutely through the rubble. Then the road began to climb, we were walking into the mountains, the ground stone-covered. Ravines opened up. I turned round, the city had already dropped out of sight; wasn't it true, then, that each convoy got its own city, or was Novorossiysk not our city? Was there a city even more destroyed? How did Kiev look, or Poltava, they must have been destroyed as well. A film came to mind: a railway line and upon it a kind of plough on wheels that tore up the tracks and ties behind it, and then I saw a dynamited dam, chunks of concrete tossed in the flood like pebbles, Bolshevism would never recover, of course Kiev was destroyed, what concern is that of mine, I thought unwillingly. We shuffled along and suddenly my gut wrenched, an animal was rooting round in there, I gave a loud groan and we shuffled up the mountains and the animal howled. The animal howled ceaselessly; then I heard, like a waterfall, the welling of a spring and bolted towards it and we fell upon spring and stream and drank them dry. 'Here camp, *spat'*, sleep!' said the senior guard, a sturdy young man with a missing left hand. I sat in the rocky grass. Shadows passed over the ravines. The senior guard took a little blue cloth out of his haversack and unknotted it. We looked at the cloth with bated breath; it could hold at most a heel of bread, too small for even two mouths, but we looked at the cloth as though it hid all the treasures of the earth. The senior guard unfolded the cloth upon the stump of his lower arm, and we saw three lumps of sugar, and the senior guard took out one lump and put it in his mouth, then reached for the second lump, but with the sweet yellow-brown lump already in his fingers, he dropped it back into the cloth and knotted it up again. The other guards gathered wood. I didn't understand what they needed a fire for, then thought perhaps we could make tea, but I wasn't familiar with the hard-stemmed plants that lifted up their clustered blue blossoms. Next to me a group of Organization Todt men lit a fire as well. I asked what they needed the fire for, and one of them mumbled that they were going to cook themselves something, then took his mess tin and walked up the mountainside, bent over, and tossed something into the mess tin now and then. It clattered; was he cooking stones? Suddenly I thought what a pity it was that you couldn't eat the earth: throw yourself down, sink your teeth in and gorge yourself, gut filled with heavy earth, the earth was our mother, why didn't she feed her children? The mess tins clattered, what were they gathering? At one hearth a pot already hung over the fire with something simmering inside, I heard the water seething, and stood up and went over, and under the steam I saw seething scum, and now I saw the bishop's-hat shapes of the bobbing shells: my comrade was cooking up a mess of snails. The guards gathered snails as well; they washed them for a long time and tossed them into boiling water, which immediately threw off scum. I didn't want to look, my hunger now a dull angry ache; I lay down again and turned out my coat and trouser pockets and rummaged through the seams for tobacco crumbs, but I'd rummaged through the seams a dozen times on the voyage, I couldn't find a single crumb. A stench seethed up. 'You gotta wait for it to boil to put the snails in, then you gotta skim off the scum, you jackasses, otherwise you're eating all the snailshit!' grumbled one of the Organization Todt men. Suddenly I longed to jump to my feet and tear up a tree and smash all of it to pieces, all of it, all of it, the snail pots and my comrades and the Russians and the still-standing walls of the city: all of it snailshit, stinking snailshit, people were nothing but snailshit, the scum of the earth, leprosy, scabs! Yes, I ought to jump up now and tear up a tree, an oak tree, and destroy everything, my stomach cried out, the snail broth spluttered over the fires, and I got up and took my mess tin and teetered up the mountain and looked for snails, but all round the mountainside was picked clean. I went to the stream and fetched water, then I looked for wood and started a fire and set the mess tin in it and then I drank hot water in tiny sips and looked at the sea and thought of all the food I'd ever turned up my nose at, and I saw white, thick, fat, fragrant food: pearl barley, plump pearl barley with meat, and we'd pulled faces at getting barley again, fish eyes, pigswill, and now I saw a trough full of barley and it stank all round like a cesspit and the fires flickered on the mountainside as the sun slowly set behind it. The guards hummed a song, the shadows grew. A steamship crossed the sea, I watched it disappear. Then I must have fallen asleep.

Next morning we moved on; the hunger had spent itself, leaving only dizziness. For several hours we walked along the mountain ridge, through trackless terrain; at last we came to a road where two rows of tents stood. Oaks lined the road, gigantic trees with ragged bark and crowns, and the mountains, now sharp peaks, glimmered purple. It must have been midday; a worker stepped out of a tent, face and hands and blouse smeared with petroleum. He spat when he saw us and said a savage word, no doubt a curse. I looked over at the mountains. '*Nu*, Fritz, where Gitler?' said the worker and spat again. We staggered along. The worker came up to us; he grabbed the man in front of me by the shoulder, and I looked at the Russian worker's hands, black, hairy, oil-smeared hands, and overcome by a wave of boundless hate I thought that these hands should be chopped off, these filthy, oil-smeared Russian hands touching the clean German uniform, and the man in front of me spun round and stared frightened into the Russian's face, and the Russian said: 'Ech, you devils—*vozmi!*', and he reached into his bag and took out a heel of black bread and handed it to the man in front of me. As I saw the bread my hunger gave another bellow. The man in front of me took the bread; like everyone else, I stared at him, willing him to share, but our comrade didn't share, he sank his teeth into the bread and stuffed the heel into his mouth with his fist and chewed with jaws stretched wide like a cobra and he gobbled down the bread and I thought, nearly screaming to myself, that I'd never have taken a Russian's filthy bread, and a shrieking saw sliced straight through my body. The road dropped down into the valley; we entered an oak forest. The road narrowed, a mule track, and then we reached a clearing where a tent stood and a draw well and a few trucks, and tall stacks of plywood panels all round. We stopped. A Russian officer came out of the tent, which had a red cross painted on a white background; he stepped before us, but we didn't see him, we were looking at the trucks loaded with potatoes and bread and burlap sacks: maybe barley, and my stomach grew hot as though something were cooking in it. In the meantime, an interpreter had stepped up and over the seething in my belly I heard him say that we had arrived at our destination and would set up camp here over the next few days, the plywood panels were for the shelters we would live in, and the interpreter said that the commander expected us to work well and fulfil and surpass our production norms to help expiate Germany's grave guilt, and then he said that in about three hours there would be soup and kasha and tobacco and sugar and bread and in the meantime our personal data would be registered and then we'd be inoculated against typhus and malaria.

Then the officer asked if there were any questions, and someone wanted to know if we would be allowed to write home, and the officer answered that soon we would, and then no one had any more questions.

We fell out; the man who had eaten the Russian bread happened to be standing next to me, and seized me by the arm. His face was pale, his breath came fast. 'Have you heard?' he breathed. 'What?' I asked. 'The shots, man, they're going to do us in!' he whispered feverishly, and I looked at him baffled; I had no idea what he was talking about. 'They're going to do us in, man!' he whispered for the third time, and he said they'd inject air into our veins, a bubble of air in the bloodstream that would enter the heart and stop it and cause a heart attack; I stared at him and said testily: 'Nonsense!' but my comrade said I should take a good look round, it was all just a mock-up to reassure us and give us the illusion that we'd arrived at a camp; he pointed round, and I saw the stacks of plywood and the tent with the red cross and the trucks with potatoes and bread and sacks, and the man next to me asked why there was nothing but silent forest round us and why the road had suddenly narrowed to a mule track and why the guards were posted all round and why they'd played the waltzes on the ship and why the Russian captain had smiled so obnoxiously and why the camp commander had just held a reassuring speech and promised us we could write home, and I heard the waltzes and saw that there was nothing but forest all round, dense, silent, Russian forest with guards posted between the trunks, and I saw the trucks camouflaged with food supplies that would drive the corpses to the ravines, and my comrade hissed in my ear: 'They're going to do us in, a shot of air in the vein or phenol straight to the heart!' My gaze strayed to the mountains, this was the Caucasus, somewhere beyond must be Turkey, the nearest civilized country, but already I heard my name.

*'Voyennoplenny Fyumann!'** the interpreter shouted, his hands cupped in front of his mouth, and mechanically I walked up to him, and the interpreter said 'Questioning!' and nodded wearily towards the tent. Now! I thought and gazed once more at the mountains, ah, Giant Mountains, blue mountains, then felt a poke in the back and stepped into the tent. Then I saw nothing more, only darkness, and heard questions, I stood utterly devoid of consciousness, and a stranger in me mechanically recited my name and my place of birth and my father's profession and the Luftwaffe Signal Corps I'd served in, and the Russian cities where I'd been stationed, and then I heard the

---

* Russian: Prisoner-of-war Fühmann.

voice ask: 'Were you a member of the NSDAP or one of its organizations?' and at that my consciousness returned. I realized without surprise that the questions had been asked in German, and now I saw my interrogator in the dim light of the tent, a Russian commissar with a typist sitting in front of him at a rough wooden table, and in the background I saw a man dressed in white doing something with syringes, and I thought: get it over with at last; let them shoot me in the head or put a rope round my neck, if only it could be over, just over with, everything over at last, and I raised my head and said loudly: 'Yes, I was in the SA!' Now the commissar had to draw his revolver, and the commissar took a step towards me and said: 'Naturally!' Naturally he'd kill me now. 'It's only natural that you were in the SA, if not in the Hitler Youth, given your youth and your social background,' said the commissar, and when he spoke I understood nothing any more; I heard his words without grasping them. I thought I heard the commissar say: 'It's a good thing you're honest!' but that just couldn't be! Then suddenly I was standing outside the tent and saw my comrades unloading bread and potatoes from the truck and saw the mountains and the oak trees and the sky above them and thought to myself that the world had gone mad, mad from this war, stark raving mad, or had I gone mad, or what was this, and cauldrons hung over

huge fires and a comrade nudged me and asked if
I'd heard yet, he had it first-hand: we'd only been
brought here to be registered because that wasn't
possible in Germany now, and right after registration we'd all be released and we'd be back home in
a fortnight!

RAINY DAY IN THE CAUCASUS
21 April 1946, Union of the KPD and SPD

It had been raining for three days now; it was an April day, and it rained as it could rain only in the Caucasus. The sky hung low, a brimming black-green duct from which the water gushed to the ground. The air was splashing wet as though within a cataract; the sky was water, the air was water, and water shot in torrents down the parade ground which sloped towards the valley, making its blue-grey clay froth like seltzer. The very first day of rain had made the parade ground and the camp road impassable; we had laid planks and trees between the barracks, the planks had sunk, only the broad-crowned oaks had held. Of course we didn't work in this weather. And so for the third day in a row we hunkered in the barracks, thinking to ourselves that the English would never manage to fly in with this rain.

We all spent our days hoping that the English would come . . . We had been in the camp here for nearly a year now, and in this time countless rumours had circulated, telling of everything from lifelong Siberian labour to immediate release; like everyone else, I had believed all these stories and angrily discarded them all when they failed to come true, but now news had come that had to be more than a rumour: it was also printed in the POW newspaper *News*. Churchill, or so I read, had held an anti-Soviet speech in the English town of Fulton,* demanding the rearmament of Germany in an attempt to extort concessions from the Soviet Union, and everyone who read that was of the same opinion as I: these concessions could only be the immediate release of the German POWs. The next day, this piece of news was filled in by Kalle, the tractor mechanic who worked outside the camp in the tent city, where he met internees from other camps: as we crowded round him that evening in the gloom of our bare wooden barrack, he reported in his slow voice that the English had given the Soviet Union an ultimatum to release the prisoners of war within fourteen days, otherwise England would use paratroopers to liberate the camps by force. These tidings coursed through our blood like rum down the throat: that was no rumour, that was no story, it had been printed in the *News*, 'extort concessions', it had said, we'd read it with our own eyes, so it had to be true. The next

---

* Referring to Churchill's 'Iron Curtain speech'; however, Fulton is actually in Missouri, USA, not England.

day the date of the imminent landing was already being whispered round, and since then, hour after hour, we'd scanned the sky for the Hurricanes' grey hulks above the purple peaks, and in our dreams we'd seen the sky over the mountains full of Hurricanes, but now the sky was a black-green duct, the rain had been pouring down for three days now, and it was clear to us that the English would never be able to fly in with this rain.

And so we hunkered in the barrack: some lay dozing on their cots; some played chess with hand-whittled pieces; some brewed tea from blackberry leaves; some scraped crumbs of tobacco from their pocket seams for the tenth time; some talked about the battles of Tobruk and Odessa, scratching situation maps on the tamped clay floor. Some read. Some were conducting an elaborate discussion about the best way to fry beefsteak, waxing lyrical about the pleasures of the mythical past. I had brewed blackberry leaf tea and sat on the cot with my friend Heinz, a twenty-five-year-old philosophy student; we sat side by side, cross-legged, sipped our tea and talked as we talked every day. 'I've been thinking about it for a long time, and now I'm positive,' said Heinz, 'all history is the pursuit of power, and all power is evil because it needs to dominate human will, and so all history as such is meaningless, because evil has no meaning!' 'That's why we're martyrs of politics,' I said.

'The thing to do is stay out of everything,' said Heinz, 'the thing to do is live somewhere by yourself, in a hole deep in the ground, or go to Tibet as a monk and then just think, do nothing but think,' and I agreed. We hunkered on the cot and drank tea and made plans for the future: let the world fight its bloody battles, it would be none of our concern, we said; empires could rise and collapse into oblivion and we wouldn't even notice them, we said, and we hunkered on our cot in the middle of the Caucasian forest and drank blackberry leaf tea and mapped out the realm of the free spirit. 'We won't read newspapers any more,' said Heinz, 'we won't go to mass meetings, we won't listen to speakers, we won't vote or support an agenda, we won't say yes to anything and we won't say no, we'll make the most radical possible leap out of history.'

'They'll never get us again, those fishers of men,' I said, 'no power in the world will ever suck us into its agenda,' and Heinz said we should swear that to one another. We did, and then we brewed more tea and talked about the best way to fry beefsteak, and Heinz talked about the battles on Crete and I spoke of Athens, the shimmering city of the goddess of wisdom, and of Attica's hills, where the grapes seethed in the sun and almonds and lemons bloomed, and then we scraped the last crumbs of tobacco from our tobacco pouches and had a little smoke, and then we dozed, and after the midday soup we read a bit, Heinz *Hunger Pastor* by Wilhelm Raabe and I *In the Land of Cockaigne* by Heinrich Mann—I had never heard his name before, but I was fascinated by the way he wrote. The camp also had books and pamphlets by Marx and Engels and Lenin and Stalin; several times I'd flipped through one of the pamphlets for fun, but soon put it down again: all they talked about was wages and prices and profit, and that didn't interest me, I was no prole! So I read *In the Land of Cockaigne*; after reading we dozed again and philosophized and waited for dinner and outside, bubbling and foaming, the torrents of rain gurgled down into the valley.

And so time passed with tormenting slowness; the evening soup was dispensed and the evening portion of bread and two spoons of sugar and, unexpectedly, tobacco and a piece of dried fish: so a truck had made it up the road despite the rain! Pleased, I took my portion from the board; I had worried that I might be sent to fetch food; due to the cloudbursts, lots had been drawn and four men chosen for the job, but fate had been merciful and I was able to stay in where it was dry. I chewed on my fish; as dusk filtered through the rain and darkness and water merged, I saw a lieutenant from the camp headquarters running up the parade ground, and quickly shouted into the barrack to report what I had seen. The lieutenant, an older man, had arrived at the camp only recently; we'd had nothing to do with him so far, but we feared him; rumour had it that he was a Jewish émigré who was simply waiting for the chance to take revenge on us. He was an unprepossessing little man of perhaps fifty-five; as I saw him running through the gate I thought he was coming to chase us out into the rain, but then I decided that he wouldn't come himself, he'd send a guard with his orders. But he was coming himself, and he was clearly in a hurry; balancing on the backs of the oaks, he charged uphill through the camp, unable to avoid slipping from the trunks, once to the left and once to the right, landing in the sea of mud and soiling his trousers over the knees. It must be something unusual, something quite extraordinary the lieutenant had to tell us, for our camp, like all the camps, was self-administered, and it was really only for the roll call that an officer from headquarters ever came to the camp. The rain splashed; we watched the officer run towards our barracks and sat up straight on our cots, and suddenly someone said: 'Churchill!' He merely voiced what we were all thinking: Churchill! He said: 'Churchill'; he didn't say it very loudly, but the word droned in our ears like the Hurricanes' propellers. Churchill, we thought, Churchill, he'll bail us out, the fine old fellow, and world history had meaning again.

'Churchill,' said Heinz now too, just as the door was flung open and the lieutenant came in, panting. He was dripping wet; his trouser legs were soaked with mud. Suddenly I felt myself trembling. 'Comrades, I have important news for you!' cried the lieutenant, still panting. He spoke without an accent. The rain splashed at the tiny window. We saw nothing but the lieutenant's face. 'Joyous news, comrades, an event of great historical importance for you,' said the lieutenant. His face shone. In that moment I saw a meadow and a spring. 'A joyous event, comrades!' the lieutenant repeated, forcing his panting lungs to voice calm speech. 'A long-standing goal in the struggle of the German working class has been achieved: in the Soviet Zone of Occupation the KPD and the SPD have joined to form the Socialist Unity Party!'*

I still saw the meadow and the spring, symbols of my desire for freedom; I'd heard his words, I didn't understand them, I heard the rain splash and suddenly there was yelling all round, the barrack yelled and I yelled too. 'Who gives a damn!' yelled one and 'Send us home already!' yelled another

---

* Many on the left blamed the Nazi's rise to power in part on the inability of the Social Democrats (SPD) and Communists (KPD) to form a 'united front' against them. In 1946, under Soviet pressure, the SPD was forced to merge with the KPD in Eastern Germany to form the Socialist Unity Party (SED).

and 'Give us something to eat instead!' yelled a third and a fourth whinnied with laughter, and everyone yelled, and Heinz yelled, and I yelled too. The rain splashed. Standing in the barracks door, the lieutenant looked at us helplessly; his gaze wandered helpless from one face to the next, and then in an infinitely hesitant gesture he lifted his shoulders and his slightly opened hands and looked at us and said: 'But the German working class is united now, comrades!' and he looked at us and we yelled in a hissing chorus. Whoever the lieutenant looked in the face stopped yelling, but the others he wasn't looking at yelled on, and the lieutenant lowered his hands, and I saw tears come to his eyes. 'I thought it would make you happy,' he said softly, and he turned on his heel and passed his hand over his eyes and went to the door. At the door he stopped; he hesitated, his hand on the wooden latch, but then he jerked the door open and went outside without turning round again. The yelling broke off, and I knew that now we were all afraid. The camp had never seen a demonstration like that before. The rain splashed.

I crouched on my cot wondering what would happen now, when my neighbour said as though in a dream: 'My god, that's what we were fighting for till 1933 . . .' What had got into my neighbour Paul? Until now he'd been one of us, he'd been captured with us and cursed the Russians with us and discussed the best way to fry beefsteak and described the fighting at Narvik, and just at lunch he'd talked about Churchill's ultimatum, but now he was one of us no longer. He crouched on his cot and stared into space, and his eyes too gleamed moistly. 'Shut up, man!' said Kalle, the tractor mechanic, whose cot was to the left of Paul's, and 'Why don't you just move to Russki-land?' I said. Paul didn't reply. He crouched on his cot and stared into space, and his lips twitched; then he gave an incomprehensible growl and lay down and pulled the blanket over his head. He pretended to sleep, but that night I saw him get up and go over to the window and stare out into the night.

I couldn't sleep either, nor could Heinz; we crouched by the stove, talking quietly. 'Those idiots actually think we give a damn about their Unity Party,' said Heinz. I nodded mutely and stared at the round black stove. 'They won't get us now,' said Heinz, 'neither of us!' 'I'll never think about politics again,' I said, 'never again!' 'Unity Party, just the sound of it!' said Heinz with contempt, looking over at Paul. 'All politics leads to massification,' he said, 'but we must maintain our individuality and never be submerged in the masses!'

The rain splashed.

'They'll never get us again,' I said, and then we talked about fried potatoes. Heinz knew a way to brown onions that I'd never heard of before. Neither of us spoke to Paul, who was one of us no longer. Gradually dawn came, and the rain gurgled. It had been raining for four days now, the sky was a tattered black-green sack, the air splashed water as though within a cataract, and it was clear to us that once again the English wouldn't manage to fly in today . . .

A DAY LIKE ANY OTHER

10 October 1946,
Sentencing at the Nuremberg Trials

It was a splendid autumn day; in the valleys the
canopies of the apple orchards blazed emerald and
wine-red; far away the glacier summits stood
orange-gold against the vast blue wall of the sky,
and even the stony slopes between summit and
valley had the silver sheen of peach fuzz. Veins of
quartz dazzled in the cliffs; the air smelt of thyme
and, though the sun still glowed warmly, of fresh
snow. It must have been about three in the afternoon, and I had just finished digging the last section of the ditch by the left shoulder of the road on
whose four, bold, uphill curves we had been working for nearly a year now, and was smoothing the
side with the shovel blade when the head engineer,
a slender captain of about sixty, with the grace of
an artist, not a soldier, gave the sign to stop work.
'Oi, so soon *rabota** kaput,' said the very young
guard, rubbing his hands happily. I climbed out of
the ditch, joined one of the loose rows that formed

---

* Russian: work.

a wobbly marching block, and wondered what had happened to make the engineer fall us in now, with a good two hours left till the end of the shift. The engineer waved the interpreter over. This was unusual as well; when the engineer had something to say to us, he told the senior camp inmate.

'The captain requests a military line-up and expects the leader of the labour company to report!' the interpreter barked. What was the idea, I thought, those kinds of shenanigans had gone out long ago! Grumbling spread and feet shuffled. Lieutenant Werner, the leader of the labour company, gave his commands, crimson-faced: sluggishly, by fits and starts, we moved into three vaguely straight lines; the lieutenant looked at us pleadingly, but we stayed where we were. Finally the lieutenant said: 'Eyes left!' and we looked over at the captain, and Lieutenant Werner reported, standing at attention. Meanwhile the engineer saluted, ramrod straight, with his hand to his cap, and then he said a few words, about *rabota* again, of course, and contrary to his usual habit he spoke in a loud martial tone. They must be having one of their days again, I thought, the Day of the Engineering Troops or the Day of the Roadbuilders or even the Day of the Prisoners of War, they had a day like that for every kind of work! Then I heard the interpreter bark that the section of the naphtha road assigned to our camp had been completed and the captain congratulated us on our good work and would recommend the best of us to the camp commander for awards! The engineer raised his hand to the brim of his cap again; stunned, Lieutenant Werner said something akin to 'Thank you, sir!' then commanded: 'Right face!' and we turned sluggishly towards the road, the guard said his '*Nu, davai!*'* and, as always, we shuffled up the road we'd slaved at for so long. The sunlight lay orange-red on the glaciers of the summits, and though the south wind warmed it, the air tasted strangely of snow.

Our section of the road was complete—it was some time before I fully grasped it. Never, I'd thought, as we faced the stone-covered slope with our tinplate spades and shovels and tested the ground's hardness with a perfunctory poke that made the shovel blade bend immediately—never, I'd thought, could we scratch out so much as a mule track with these tools, and I'd thought our assignment was nothing but a bad joke or a bureaucrat's plan, dreamt up at the drawing board, and when two men with a tripod, level and levelling rod actually began surveying the path of the road which would open up new petroleum fields, I laughed grimly at the insane

---

* Russian: Come on!

notion of building a road through stony ground with nothing but tinplate and a pair of hands. Then we'd commenced work, the shovel blades had bent, some broke; we'd fought for the few pickaxes and made ourselves crowbars of wood; even in that icy winter the sweat dripped from our brows, and I thought to myself that the road whose band edged so slowly, oh so snail-like up the slope, must taste salty from all the sweat and bitter from all the curses it had drunk, but slowly, metre by metre, the road had grown; once it shot forward, as we dug through a pocket of sand, and once it stopped short when we hit a vein of blue-grey mud which we merely churned with our shovel blades, unable to scoop it up, finally forced to scrape it out with our bare hands; we'd slaved away at the road like that for nearly a year, autumn, winter, spring, summer and September again, and now September was past and our section was complete, how had that happened? But it was a fact: our road was complete, trucks drove past, here had been the vein of mud we'd had to scrape out with our bare hands, and now the trucks drove where the blue naphtha mud had stretched, and the road held up, it didn't cave in, its bed didn't yield, its surface didn't crack, and against my will a sense of pride came over me. I noticed it when I suddenly stopped dragging my feet across the road surface as usual without lifting them, and strode along more vigorously, as though

I trusted its solidity; in spite of myself I looked round and saw that the others were walking more freely as well and raising their heads, and someone even cracked a joke. So you're finished after all, you bastard, I thought almost tenderly, looking at the road. It gleamed dully in the afternoon sun, a dark band upon the mountain. You goddamned bastard, I thought, and realized to my surprise that I was proud.

Like all the others, I usually trudged home in sullen silence after work, but now I felt the need to chat, and looked round for Major Hochreither. I couldn't talk to Heinz, who was no longer in my company; weeks ago he had managed to find a coveted place in the forest detachment which gathered mushrooms, berries and wild fruit: plums, apples and luscious, palm-sized *beurre gris* pears which often covered the moss ankle-deep; sometimes he brought me a handful. I was no longer on good terms with Heinz, either; he had tried to convince me to do as he did, ingesting excessive amounts of salt and standing for hours each night so as to retain water in the legs, get assigned to the easiest work detachment and maybe even get priority release in a few weeks; I had refused, and Heinz had said scornfully that freedom meant taking risks. And so I had gravitated towards Major Hochreither, son of a famous linguist, a cultivated man of about forty who, like few at that time, had foregone his officer's privilege to be released from work and worked on the road with us for the past year. I liked him, and he seemed to like me too; after work we often ate our evening soup together, leaning against the western wall of the barracks in the sunshine and chatting about this and that, and sometimes I read him the poems I had scratched with an ink pencil stub on one of the beech shingles that stood in for precious paper in camp correspondence, poems I had to scratch away again with a shard of glass when the shingle was full. Major Hochreither nearly always praised my poems, which mostly mourned a lost paradise and yearned for the freedom of gentler climes; of one, an elegy to Europa on the bull, he even claimed that several lines came close to Weinheber, and I was very proud at his praise, for Josef Weinheber, the lonely Viennese poet, had always been my poetic idol. And so I kept an eye out for Major Hochreither as we left the road to take a shortcut across a trackless, hilly plateau, its stony ground blotched blue-black with petroleum swamps like a beaten body. Far away at the edge of the plateau I saw an oil rig propelled forward, a dot moving round at its vertiginous tip; astonished, I stopped in my tracks. Did the oil rig have wheels? Was it gliding on rails? How else could it move, especially on this hilly terrain? The guards and the rest of the column had stopped as well, staring at the distant

oil rig; slowly the rig came closer, and now I saw
that each of its steel feet rested on two crawler
tractors coupled together, directed by a man
who drove on ahead of the skyscraper in a cross-
country vehicle, waving red and blue flags. It was
a fascinating picture: the tower veered quivering
like a seismograph needle when the earth splits
open; it swung far to both sides in a huge semicircle, and my breath caught when I looked up at the
red-flag-waving man who swayed at the very top
of the rig like an ear of grain on its knotty stalk.
Slowly the gigantic team of eight drew near. The
tractors stopped at the edge of a naphtha pool,
where the ground just barely bore the iron weight.
The man who had given directions jumped out of
his vehicle with the bundle of flags, and now, far
away, I saw a long line of men carrying something
glittery, steel cables or perhaps rails, on their shoulders. The line approached the rig like a procession;
the whole scene could have been taken from the
Iliad.

Major Hochreither nudged me. 'Marvellous,
eh?'

I nodded.

'Amazing, the way they solve their technical
problems with the most primitive means,' said
Major Hochreither.

I merely shrugged my shoulders, gazing at
the oil rig. The worker scrambled down. He was

young, with a dashing moustache. He laughed, and the others laughed too.

'*Nu davai, kamerad, domoi!*'* said the guard, and we trudged onward.

Major Hochreither walked by my side. 'Do you have it yet?' he asked.

'What?' I asked distractedly, still seeing the swaying rig with its flag-waving freight.

'The book, what else?' said Major Hochreither; now I understood, and I said I'd only received it three days ago and would finish reading it today and give it to him tomorrow. Since the end of August, when four crates of German books had arrived at the camp for the second time, a book was being passed secretly from hand to hand, now thoroughly tattered; it had to be a mistake that it had ended up in our camp library and been lent out to us. It was a novel about Russian working life in the 1920s, written by a Russian who clearly knew his stuff, a certain Ilya Ehrenberg or Ehrenstadt or something like that, who described the building of a blast furnace plant near a town called Kuznetsk with such incredible openness that it had to have got him hanged:** the author describes

* Russian: Come on, comrade, let's go home!
** *The Second Day* (1933) by Ilya Ehrenburg (1891–1967); in fact, Ehrenburg initially had trouble publishing the work in the Soviet Union and it ultimately appeared in a censored version.

how a country that had ousted its educated class attempts to build a blast furnace plant in the middle of Siberia lacking the most rudimentary technical means; the people, men and women alike, live in earthen huts; some of the workers are semi-savages who can't even read or write; feral children roam the country, scuffling over a half-rotten apple next to a wooden shack, a so-called club, where someone gives a speech on the joys of Communism; one worker's fingers freeze off, another is squashed by a primitive crane—this book had fallen into our hands by mistake, that was the only explanation, and if the Russians got wind of its existence they'd confiscate it at once!

Meanwhile we had reached one of the swamps that could be forded; steadying ourselves with one of the oak sticks that lay piled at the edge of the ford, we balanced our way along the vault of an iron pipe half a metre wide that stretched forty metres to the other side. Cursing to myself as always at this spot, I was slowly placing foot in front of foot on the slick metal when I saw a column of trucks on the other side of the ford, carrying floodlights to the oil rig, and I thought to myself that they'd be working day and night again, as they so often did, and as I thought this I recalled a scene in the novel that I hadn't understood. One of the workers building the smelting works was Volodya, a student, and this Volodya had been expelled from the Komsomol for some mistake or offence I hadn't entirely grasped, and had to leave the construction site and return to Moscow, and instead of leaping with joy in his smoky earthen hut, Volodya was crushed and wept and begged to be allowed to stay and prove himself through his work, and I simply didn't understand. I thought about my time in the Labour Service—my god, I would have gone home on foot and barefoot at that, if only I could have escaped, and this Volodya even got a train ticket to Moscow and was unhappy about it, what in heaven's name was that all about? Why did they willingly endure their earthen dens, why was Volodya unhappy that he couldn't stay in Hell, why did they work at night in the floodlights without grumbling instead of starting one of those revolutions they were always having, and as I pondered I slipped on the slope of the pipe and just managed to catch myself with the oak stick, otherwise I would have sprawled into the sludge. Angrily I balanced the last few metres to the edge of the ford, and when Major Hochreither joined me again and said he was reading Lenin's essays on Tolstoy and advised me to read them too, it was quite astonishing what a materialist like Lenin, who oughtn't to be capable of recognizing soul or intellect, had to say about Tolstoy, I gave a sullen, taciturn reply; I had my own problems, I was already getting far too caught up with these Russian questions!

Then we reached our road again and trudged through an oak forest to the camp. I stopped short: over the camp gate hung a wooden sign with the hastily painted words: 'GLORY TO THE WERNER LABOUR SQUAD FOR COMPL-', but the painter had come no further. Next to the gate stood the camp commander and the engineer, who must have driven on ahead in a truck, and a bulky gramophone blared out some crackling Russian march. I stared at the sign like an imbecile. Since when was I a shock worker* with honour and glory, that was political, that was the last thing in the world I wanted to be! The camp tailors, sitting in the sun patching coats outside the services building, gave us dirty looks. The camp commander gave a speech; we'd done credit to anti-fascist Germany, he said, and I wondered angrily what that was supposed to mean, I was a German, I didn't want to be an anti-fascist, and then the commander said that tomorrow we'd all get a double helping of soup and kasha for lunch, and at that my ears perked up again. Then we fell out; I sat on my cot and read the rest of the novel, and when I'd finished it I thought to myself that they'd pulled off their converter in Kuznetsk after

---

* From Russian *udarnik*, the term for highly productive Soviet workers.

all, just as we'd pulled off our section of road, and I caught myself feeling happy for them. Then Heinz came; he emptied four pockets full of fruit onto the cot, mostly *beurre gris* pears, but he didn't give me a single pear, he tossed me two crab apples and asked me if we'd gone mad, playing shock workers for the Russkis, and I said that it wasn't my fault and I was glad we wouldn't have to go back to that section of the road, and as I spoke I felt that idiotic pride again. Meanwhile I munched on the crab apples; they were bitter and tasted of ink, but I munched them greedily. A Hungarian who worked in the kitchen—our camp had Hungarians and Rumanians as well—came into the barrack and went up to Heinz and handed him a bulging little sack. Heinz felt it, then pointed to the cot, and the Hungarian stowed the pears in his cap and left. Our comrades, who had stared greedily at Heinz's pears, turned away in disappointment. I saw that Heinz would give me nothing any more, but I couldn't blame him: everyone bartered, why should Heinz be the do-gooder?

'You'll get pears again tomorrow,' said Heinz and packed a pipe he'd whittled.

'Tobacco?' I asked, pointing to the sack, and Heinz said he was going to barter his dinner for tobacco, this sack had salt in it. Then he took his mess tin, a leaky can patched with clay at the seam between side and bottom, exactly the kind I had, and went to the well. I knew he was going to drink litres of salt water now and spend half the night dangling his legs from the cot so that the water would sink into the tissues of the legs and cause an oedema; rumour had it that the worst-afflicted prisoners had already been released. When the rumour reached the camp that prisoners with oedemas were given priority for release, I, like most, had procured salt and choked down brine, but it had made me so sick that I abandoned that experimental path towards freedom and decided to work on the road instead. Heinz returned, his twisted face and half-open mouth showing that he'd already downed the salt. Water sloshed in his mess tin. There was a racket outside; the last detachment, the brickmakers, was marching in. Meanwhile Heinz had sat down on the cot and rolled up his trouser legs; now he pressed the tip of his right index finger into the flesh of his thigh above the knee, evidently with little force, and looked with satisfaction at the deep indentation that remained in the waterlogged, waxen tissue like a footprint in moist clay, slow to close.

'I'll be home in a month,' he said.

'Or six feet under!' said I.

'Freedom means taking risks!' said Heinz, and then, as though goaded by my question, he flung up his head and yelled, launching the words like projectiles, that he wasn't planning to spend his life rotting in the Caucasus; the Russkis were just going to let us croak, he yelled, and he yelled in my face that certain scoundrels were stabbing their comrades in the back and doing shock work for the Russkis, and then he lowered his voice and jumped up and hissed that those scoundrels would be dealt with back home, all right, and Germany would be on its feet again one day, we could bet our lives on it, and it would be on the march again, and one day everyone who'd betrayed his people to the Russians would go on trial, everyone, everyone, everyone, and Heinz shook his fists and a thread of spittle ran from his mouth. My fists itched, I longed to punch him in the face, but I pulled myself together and went outside. 'You won't get another pear from me, you dog!' Heinz yelled, and I yelled that I didn't give a damn about his pears, and went out and slammed the barrack door behind me.

The sun was setting; incandescent clouds had gathered about the mountains, resting like velvet on the crowns of the oaks. I gazed towards the homeland I didn't even know; I was one of the few who had received no letters yet, and I didn't know whether my family was still alive or if they had been resettled, and if so, where. Down on the road the trucks rolled past, no doubt driving to the oil rig; so they were working all night again. Would we work with them tomorrow? We would see; one more day had passed; a day like any other, I thought wearily, one of the eternally identical days since the beginning of our internment: get up, wash, roll call, work, eat, and now sleep without dreams; it was always the same, each day was identical, an identical sequence of identical days, and no change in sight. Of course the road was completed, but that was bound to happen; everything is finished at some point, even such a road, and one day this internment would pass as well, this time of internment that unrolled in monotonous-grey sameness, this dead stretch of a human life, as monotonous as a Russian snowfield!

The guard plodded by the barbed-wire fence. Thinking of all the sentry duty I'd had as a soldier, I didn't envy him. Nice guys really, these Russkis, I thought, and was reflecting on how decent it was of them not to make us work day and night, as they themselves did, when I heard voices and steps on the camp road. It was Kalle and Paul, returning home from the mechanic's workshop. They were talking loudly, probably another fight about their politics, which I wanted nothing to do with.

I went up to them. 'What's up?' I asked.

'Sentencing in Nuremberg,' said Paul, shifting his hammer to the other shoulder.

'Well?' I said, just to have something to say.

'Most of them will be hanged!' said Kalle.

'They sure had it coming,' I said, and Paul and Kalle nodded.

7 October 1949,
The Founding of the German Democratic Republic

I witnessed the founding of the German Democratic Republic as a teaching assistant at an anti-fascist school in Latvia—still a Soviet POW, but freer than ever before. I had come to the school in the autumn of 1947, and with the introductory courses on political economy the scales fell from my eyes: here was the answer to all the questions that drove me, and as I burrowed through the thick volumes of Karl Marx's *Capital*, the stations of my life appeared, tangible as the desk where I sat, and my eyes now saw clearly, down into the depths of time. The course had lasted half a year, and then I was asked whether I wanted to go home or stay on at the school as an assistant, and I stayed, gazing from afar at a Germany that was as close and dear to me as never before, and watching indignantly as the old seed of ruin shot up again in one part of Germany and this one Germany seceded from the other and drove wedge after wedge between German and German. Bizone, Trizone, currency reform, separate state;* those were reports

---

* Bizone was a combination of the US and British zones of
occupation in Germany in 1947, joined in 1948 by the French

that robbed us of our sleep, but now good news had come: in the east of Germany the people were building their own state.

It was a bright October morning; we watched the Latvian farmers walk past the blue camp fence to work as they did early every day; then we sat crowded round the loudspeakers in the barracks, and at noon Latvian Young Pioneers came to congratulate us on the birth of the democratic German state. With flaxen hair, clear eyes, enormous bouquets of red and yellow flowers in their arms, they came down the camp road, and in front of the picture of Wilhelm Pieck* on the facade of the House of Culture they nudged one another and said: 'Wilhelm Pieck—Wilhelm Pieck!', and a snub-nosed girl cried: 'Wilhelm Pieck—hurraah!' and all the children cried: 'Wilhelm Pieck—hurraaah!' and waved the big red and yellow bouquets. Tears rose to our eyes; we had never seen anything like it. We stood shyly, almost helplessly, before these Latvian children who were crying hurrah for the president of a German Republic; for several moments we stood there moist-eyed, and then the children rushed towards us and embraced us and thrust their bouquets into our arms. In the evening

---

zone, making the Trizone. Currency reform: introduced in the western zones of occupation in 1948.

* Wilhelm Pieck (1876–1960): served as the only president of the GDR from 1949 until his death.

the farmers came to pick up their children, and one of the farmers came through the camp gate and shook our hands. It was the first time one of these farmers had given us his hand. He said: '*Auf Wiedersehn!*' in harsh, broken German, then turned, as though he'd already said too much, and walked away. The children waved. From that day on I knew: no matter where in Germany I'd live, this republic was my republic!

Our school was dissolved in mid-December 1949. The journey, in freight cars, was a long one. On 22 December we arrived at the Gronefelde release camp near Frankfurt an der Oder, and on 24 December, now a citizen of the German Democratic Republic, I travelled to Berlin to continue from there to Weimar, where, as I had learnt, my mother and sister were staying.

All I owned then was fifty marks in cash; a suit and a coat, both tailored from dyed Wehrmacht uniforms; a pair of heavy shoes; a fur hat; some underwear; soap and a toothbrush; a set of cutlery; three pamphlets; and a wooden suitcase filled with the treasures I'd managed to purchase from my wages before leaving Latvia: a tin of coffee blend, a piece of smoked meat, canned fish, cigarettes, sugar, cocoa. But the greatest treasure I had acquired during my internment was what I carried in my head: a new, valid worldview.

Now I was in the train, heading for Berlin. I stood wedged in a crowd of tired, nervous, irritable people; the train panted and huffed asthmatically; the air was heavy with sweat and coal slack; I daydreamt. I daydreamt about the hour of reunion and about the new life ahead, and between the headscarves and lumpy caps of my fellow passengers I saw a narrow strip of grey flat land; that, then, was Germany; for the first time I saw the land east of the Oder. It was grey and flat, I saw a brook with willows and alders, puddles on the fields, flying crows. Suddenly the train stopped; we were jumbled together, men cursed and women scolded; an elaborate process of document and luggage checks began, and word went out that we were just outside Berlin. I managed to worm my way over to a window. The train rode on; now I saw sparse woods, mostly pines and birches, then grey land, criss-crossed by cobbled roads, edged by allotment gardens, summerhouses with crooked walls and tattered pasteboard roofs, and then the grey land fell behind and the wasteland began. Brick rubble lay before our eyes, red-brown, blackened, and still exhaled the smell of burning. It was a wasteland, a wasteland of rubble. I shivered. I thought of Novorossiysk; that had been a destroyed city, but this was a city no longer, this was pulverized stone. 'Berlin,' breathed one of my comrades whose home these ruins had been. He turned away. So this was Berlin, these were its eastern districts, and the deserted railway station through which the train crept, without roof or lighting, was called Silesian Station. The train moved sickeningly slow, and I had just one thought in my mind: never to have to live in this field of rubble. 'That won't be cleaned up in a hundred years,' my comrade said hollowly. The bricks stank of ash and burning. Crows wheeled. Dust rose from the rubble. I stood in silence.

Friedrichstrasse Station was the end of the line. It was late in the morning, almost noon, but my train to Weimar didn't leave until evening. And so I decided to visit an acquaintance, the only person I knew in Berlin: the friend who had read a poem of mine and advised me to study the Edda. I recalled his old address in Zehlendorf, in the west of Berlin, and rode out there on an off-chance. The address was still current, a small but elegant villa.

'Good god!' cried my acquaintance, a gentleman of about forty, smart and well-dressed, once I had introduced myself. He stared at me thunderstruck. 'Then you escaped from that Russian hell?'

'So you see,' I said.

'And of course you'll be hurrying straight on to the West,' he cried, dragging me into the house.

'No, not at all,' I said.

'But you'll hardly get a residency permit for West Berlin,' he said.

'I don't want to move here, either,' I said.

'Are you planning to emigrate?' he asked in surprise.

'No, not at all, I'm going to Weimar,' I said.

He dropped my hand and cried: 'But surely you won't go back to the Russian zone of your own free will, now that you're safe!'

I laughed.

'I'm going to live in the German Democratic Republic, of course,' I said, and my acquaintance stared at me again as though he doubted my sanity. Then he seemed to have an idea. He went away, came back with a laden tray and began setting the table without a word. In eloquent silence he set out milk and honey, butter, pastries, rolls, candies, chocolate, ham, sausage, liver pâté—a colourful array—and finally he poured black coffee. 'NESCAFÉ,' he said. 'Are you familiar with NESCAFÉ?'

I had to admit I wasn't.

He shook his head regretfully and said: 'Oh, NESCAFÉ!' His face was transfigured, he was working on an ode. 'NESCAFÉ!' he said, 'the best coffee in the world, simply fabulous, an American product, you just toss the coffee powder into boiling water and it dissolves completely! No pesky filters, no grounds, no sediment, clear, black, strong coffee, better than machine-brewed— splendid, isn't it?'

'Really quite practical,' I said.

'NESCAFÉ,' he said again, and, holding the little tin between his right thumb and middle finger, he flicked his left index finger to make it spin, glinting silver. Then he set the tin solemnly next to my cup, gestured towards the richly laid table and said: 'Well!' Nothing but: 'Well!' Clearly he thought this culinary argument would bowl me over. I buttered a roll and asked him about private matters. He replied in monosyllables. As I bit into my roll, he said reproachfully: 'How can you possibly want to go to the Russian zone, you don't even know the place!'

'Oh yes I do,' I said, 'I've been paying close attention to the developments leading to the Federal Republic here and the German Democratic Republic there; I've examined both governments' agendas, and . . .'

'But that's politics, that's humbug!' he exclaimed heatedly, piling whipped cream onto his NESCAFÉ. 'Really, my dear fellow, that's humbug, what matters is how you live!'

'Precisely,' I said, 'but for me that means more than consuming whipped cream and NESCAFÉ!'

'Me too,' he said, 'freedom, for instance!'

'Freedom, for instance,' I said, 'the question is, for whom!'

'For the mind,' he said, and, evidently seized by a new idea, he took me into an adjoining room and showed me his library with the same gesture as when he'd said 'Well!' and pointed towards the laden table. This time he didn't say 'Well!' He merely pointed towardss the bookcase, and there they were, in rank and file, the testaments to his freedom: Eliot, Camus, Pound and many others I didn't know; among them, lo and behold, were Binding and Jünger, and them I knew. I read the titles and authors as my acquaintance waited silently. Finally he did say 'Well!' 'Well!' he said, 'What do you say to that? You'll never see that in the Russian zone?'

'Certainly not Binding and Jünger,' I said, 'and that's absolutely right!'

He didn't think that was right. He also found Jünger macabre, he said, and of course Binding had had fateful ties with National Socialism, but both of them were part of German cultural history, and that was what freedom meant, letting men like that have their say as well. I asked him about Marx and Lenin and Sholokhov, and he turned indignant, and for the third time he said 'Well!' 'Well,' he said, 'you'll get the ideology out of your system soon enough, life itself will convince you: in a year at most your Russian zone will be in shards!'

I smiled.

Suddenly he took my hand again. 'I know you're very eastern-oriented, you're impressed by the Russians, that was clear even during the war, I can understand that,' he said, 'but you're an intelligent person, you'll have no scope for action there!'

'I'm convinced of the opposite,' I said, and tried to explain that the study of Marxism had illuminated the stations of my life for me and that my internment had given meaning to my existence.

Now it was he who smiled. 'Those are the usual phrases,' he said, making a gesture as if to wipe something away, 'those are the usual phrases when people get new notions,' he said, pushing a piece of apple cake towards me, 'in a year you'll think differently, my dear fellow, by then you'll have got to know your new state quite well.' He looked at me sharply. 'And then I'll be there for you as if nothing had happened!' he said slowly.

I got up. It was not just time that was running out.

'Will you write poems again?' he asked.

'Certainly,' I said, though I wasn't sure of it yet. Since enrolling at the school I hadn't written another line.

'You know, you should write a danse macabre, that would be just your thing, a ghoulish, demonic danse macabre reflecting the entire apocalypse of our day,' he said, and finished his NESCAFÉ. 'The entire apocalypse,' he said, setting down his cup, 'the existential loneliness, the despair, the implacability, the thrownness* . . .' He wiped the whipped cream from his lips. 'Won't you at least take some sandwiches?' he asked. I declined politely and left. From the window, leaning far over the railing, he called after me: 'Remember the danse macabre—I promise to look for a publisher!'

There was a wait at the Zehlendorf station. I went up to a kiosk and skimmed the newspapers that hung there. It took my breath away. At school, lecturers returning from Germany had told us about the anti-Soviet agitation in West Germany; now I saw it with my own eyes, for the first time since the Goebbels era, and saw Goebbels resurrected. I was disgusted: what vulgarities, what filth, what lies! I felt physically ill. At last the train came and took me back to Friedrichstrasse Station, and now, for the second time this Christmas season, I had a sense of homecoming: I had come home to my Republic. I looked round: the grey station with its grey windows; a tiny Christmas tree, flags and banners, hurrying people, a newsstand. I went over. 'What's new?' I asked the man at the kiosk.

---

* Thrownness: term introduced by philosopher Martin Heidegger to describe the experience of being 'thrown' into the world and situations beyond one's control.

He looked me up and down, standing in my dyed uniform, the fur *shapka* on my head, the wooden suitcase clamped between my legs, clumsily counting the unfamiliar money. 'What's new with the Russkis?' he asked back in a growl, and he spat when I said 'Lots of good things!', and made a face. He doesn't like us, I thought, and I looked at the newspapers he sold, and I saw that even if he didn't like us, he had to sell newspapers that told the truth. That seemed like a good thing to me, and I thought that daily dealings with the truth would transform him as well, just as truth experienced daily had transformed us, who three years ago (was it really just three years ago?) had been fascists. I bought a *Neues Deutschland*, a *BZ am Abend* and a magazine, and I read and waited, and then five o'clock was long past and the train to Erfurt arrived, very late.

The train was only moderately full—it was Christmas Eve, after all—and I actually got a seat. I shared a compartment with a police officer and her children, boys of seven and nine. She was a homely, big-boned woman, but when she looked out the window I gazed at her furtively; it was a long time since I'd seen a woman so close. Then we got into a conversation; her husband, she told me, had been killed in the Neuengamme concentration camp in 1944: an SS specialist had smashed the vertebrae of his neck with a wooden stick. She explained candidly that she'd always been what she called apolitical, but after her husband's death she had sworn to fight his murderers, and had applied to the police force. Now an officer of the German People's Police, raising her children alone, she was going to spend the Christmas holidays in a recreation home that had once been the castle of a Thuringian count. Once again the journey dragged on with tormenting slowness: elaborate baggage inspections, half-hour waits between stations, and in Weissenfels the half-empty train was suddenly thronged to bursting. Crowds of noisy men pressed through the doors and climbed through the windows, suitcases and rucksacks were passed along overhead, and in the wink of an eye the conductor was trapped in the corridor. All the people crowding in were workers, most of them slightly tipsy, roaring with laughter and joking as they spread out among the compartments until everyone had more or less found a place. The workers unpacked their rucksacks: bread, big chunks of sausage, a piece of butter, a slab of bacon, bottles of vodka, corn schnapps and kummel, and began eating dinner. Each one was eating far more than the weekly ration you could purchase with ration cards; it had to be from the HO shops,* and if it

---

* HO: 'Handelsorganisation' (Trade Organization), a state-run retail organization founded in 1948 in the GDR, offering non-rationed, higher-priced goods.

was HO goods, then each was consuming twice the cash I possessed. They were Wismut miners, the police officer told me, underground miners, the best-paid workers in the Republic. The miners began singing wistful Christmas songs; the land outside lay in profound darkness, and the dim little lamp dangling from the ceiling spent its yellow light helplessly in the gloom.

And so we trundled along in the gloom; a miner offered me sausage and brandy; I drank, though I hadn't had alcohol in years. To get some fresh air I wormed my way into the corridor to a broken window where the wind whistled through, and there, at the window, at the gaping hole in the pane, stood a man, clearly a returning soldier like myself. The man stood almost motionless, eyes wide, and stared steadily into the blackness of this Christmas night, his hands clutching the sliding window's sooty grip. I overcame my shyness and spoke to him. Gradually a conversation developed; he told me that he was a returnee from a Soviet POW camp, and now he was going home, where he, the former farmhand of a Thuringian country squire, had received land through the agrarian reform, his own land, for once in his life his own land, and he told me that his wife had been farming the land, and he told me about cropping plans and targets and seedtime and harvest and machines, and tomorrow, tomorrow at the crack of dawn he'd be standing on land of his own! He stared out into the night, the icy wind whistled through the hole in the pane, and suddenly I knew: this would be a poem! and it was a poem. It was the first poem I wrote since attending the school; I wrote it in my mind as the train rattled and trundled along, and it turned out as a bright poem after all the dark poems I'd written before:

A New Farmer's Homecoming

Sturdy and square at the window he stands
To gaze at the land, the rolling expanse.
This land, this land, this black, heavy loam,
Which once in dreams did call him home,
As he sowed wheat on strangers' fields,
Strange masters' furrows, seed and yields,
As he was enslaved still, docile as cattle,
No longer a man, chattel among chattel,
In a fleeting dream he saw it then:
His own land tilled by his own hand,
With his own team and his own plough.
Land, oh land, sufficed for all, but how:
Land was *Lebensraum* and with slave masses
    teemed.
Land, oh land, yet only a dream.

Till the time of the great change drew near,

The slaves', the farmers' greatest year.

'Here, see this land, it's yours to take!

Your property! You're the master—awake!'

Now he stands there, sturdy and stark,

Travelling now through his land, through his
  March,

Coming home as his own squire.

His mouth twitches strangely, his eyes afire.

Two others have joined him, sturdy and stout.

Behold them by the window, staring out.

Behold the land, their sacred, native soil,

Behold their hands, heavy, used to toil,

Behold: the former slave comes home!

Behold and understand this: ne'er again to
  roam!

No, I thought as I finished the last line of the poem, nor shall I roam again! The train stamped and huffed, the little oil lamp smoked, from the compartment came snoring and singing, and I thought back on my life: when had it come, the initial impulse of the transformation I had undergone? At the Antifa school, where the scales fell from my eyes as I learnt to recognize society's laws of motion and, for the first time, German history's twisted path through World War and Stalingrad to the German Republic that was now my home? Certainly, that was where the transformation took place, but the impulse had to lie deeper. When I read Lenin for the first time? When I saw the crushed seashell of Novorossiysk across the harbour's brackish water? When I fled through Bohemia's forests? When I lay on my cot and heard the voice from Stalingrad resounding from the loudspeaker? Or deeper, still deeper? I didn't know, and I still don't know today; perhaps a person spends all his life journeying towards the being he could be, whom perhaps he first glimpsed with the wondering eyes of a child in the tiled stove's mirroring green.

Here the reader finds the fourteen episodes of *The Jew Car* presented for the first time in the full cycle's original form. The previously published version followed the recommendations of my then-editors, who regarded the first version as unreadable. Today I find it's the other way round, but my authorities at the time managed to convince me, and I might add: they had an easy time of it. Probably even while writing I began to sense the stylistic inconsistency in this work, expression of a fractured mindset, a switch from self-irony to affirmative pathos that had to lead to a decline in literary quality such as that between the first and the last story; the editorial suggestions aimed to adjust the inconsistency, albeit downwards. But even today I resist the temptation to mutilate or rework this cycle whose methodical eclecticism soon pained me, that is, to bring the first aesthetic reflection on my place in the new society up to the level of a second and a third, instead of achieving the second and third by living and writing more consciously and leaving the first for what it was: a stage. In an author's process of self-discovery, old works can be corrected only through new ones, provided that they are indeed new, that is, to speak with Brecht: provided that development has taken place. That the reader may decide. The ultimate goal of my literary efforts would be to depict someone I could discover to be me. No doubt I will never achieve it to the degree that I both desire and fear: the main problem is not the external censor, but the internal one. Incidentally, the identical nature of these two arbiters (there are various names for this phenomenon of congruence; it is also the ideal of a certain aesthetic) is *The Jew Car*'s ultimate flaw. It arose from the doubtless sincere belief that experience can be delegated, another remarkable phenomenon. It is a programmed way of experiencing: something evoked by ideology as an experience the future has in store for you is felt after the fact to be the most intrinsic part of you; strange self-affirmation of one who has not yet found himself. Something analogous then happens in memories: what became essential to you, you remember experiencing as essential, and indeed you did experience it, just not in those terms. Nothing here is falsified, only selected; nothing added, only omitted, and both these things are necessary. Every poetics teaches that you must select and omit. But we will speak of this many times to come.

Franz Fühmann, 1979

(afterword to the 2nd edition of *Das Judenauto*)[1]

Franz Fühmann's critique of his own breakthrough work *The Jew Car* (*Das Judenauto*), seventeen years after its first publication, says a great deal about him—more, perhaps, than about the book itself, one of the classic treatments of the psychology of Nazism. His words from 1979 reflect the 'uncompromising nature . . . tenacious and implacable' which so 'awed' his colleague Christa Wolf: the centrality of self-discovery, its painful intensity and his bracing belief in the process itself. In *The Jew Car*, Fühmann sought to fit the radical transformations of his youth—from fervent

---

1 Franz Fühmann, *Werkausgabe in 8 Bänden*, Volume 3: *Das Judenauto* (Rostock: Hinstorff Verlag, 1993), pp. 517–19. Cited with the permission of Hinstorff Verlag.

Catholic to fanatical Nazi to ardent Communist—
into one neat narrative arc. Yet the happy end is like
a hastily built dam, unable to contain the stories'
dynamic of disillusionment; following religious
and fascist fever dreams, this 'new, valid image of
the world' seems next in line to be swept away. The
narrative turns out to be open-ended. *The Jew Car*
does not merely describe a process; it writes a
process that continues past its end. By 1979, reject-
ing notions of narrative and ideological closure,
Fühmann could fully embrace the implications of
its final words: 'Perhaps a person spends all his life
journeying towards the being he could be.'

The Jew Car closely follows the initial twists of this
path. Fühmann was born in 1922 in Rochlitz an der
Iser/Rokytnice nad Jizerou in the 'Sudetenland', a
predominantly German region of Czechoslovakia.
'[The] landscape,' he later wrote, 'is home to fairy
tales.'[2] It was also home to ethnic tensions of devastating historical consequence. Fühmann's father,
Josef Rudolf, ran a small pharmaceutical factory. A
culturally active bon vivant, he was one of the town's
most prominent citizens, and a fateful presence in
Franz's life, idolized, then demonized. He encouraged his son's precocious literary talent—as well as

---

2 Hans Richter, *Franz Fühmann. Ein deutsches Dichterleben*
(Berlin: Aufbau Verlag, 2001), p. 96.

a virulent strain of Sudeten-German nationalism, for which Franz later resen-ted him. While his 'sentimental, religious'[3] mother Margaretha seems to have loomed less large in Franz's life, her Catholicism, with its emphasis on sin and confession, shaped him as a person and a writer. In 1932 his parents sent him to the prestigious Jesuit boarding school of Kalksburg, near Vienna. Austria's dominant politician was Engelbert Dollfuss, who seized dictatorial power in 1933, several months after Hitler. An Austrofascist, Dollfuss resisted Nazi attempts to gain influence in Austria, but also suppressed Austrian Social Democrats and Communists (the 'Commune'). In February 1934 the Social Democrats offered armed resistance, leading to the several-day 'Austrian Civil War' whose Vienna skirmishes could be heard in Kalksburg ('Prayers to Saint Michael').

Fühmann soon chafed under the rigorous Kalksburg discipline. His departure in 1936 appears to have been less dramatic than described in *The Jew Car*, but he did leave as a 'convinced atheist'.[4] Fourteen years old, he was sent to school in Reichenberg (the later capital of the Reichsgau Sudetenland), where he lived on his own for the first time—and was drawn into the Sudeten Fascist

3 Ibid., p. 98.
4 Ibid., p. 101.

movement ('The Defence of the Reichenberg Gymnasium'). A pivotal event for 'German brothers and sisters beyond the borders of the Reich' was the July 1938 Greater German Gymnastics and Sports Festival in Breslau (then Germany, now Wrocław, Poland), staged as a celebration of ethnic German minorities in other countries and as an appeal for a Greater Germany that would incorporate them. That October, as per the Munich Agreement, Germany annexed the Sudetenland ('Down the Mountains') and Fühmann joined the SA at the unusually young age of sixteen. In this capacity, as he later admitted, he took part in the anti-Semitic pogroms of the so-called Reichskristallnacht in November.[5]

In the summer of 1939, German–Polish tensions came to a head; the main bone of contention was Poland's 'corridor' to the Baltic, which separated East Prussia from the rest of Germany. As in the Sudetenland, Hitler accused the Poles of atrocities against their German minority. On 31 August, German forces posing as Poles staged an attack on the German radio station of Gleiwitz in Poland, offering Germany the excuse to invade Poland ('A World War Breaks Out'). Fühmann volunteered for the Wehrmacht, but was rejected for being too young. In 1941 he was admitted to the 'Reichsarbeitsdienst'

---

5 Ibid., p. 110.

or Reich Labour Service, an auxiliary force which supplied the Wehrmacht troops and performed construction work. On 22 June 1941, his unit accompanied the Wehrmacht on its surprise invasion of the Soviet Union ('Catalaunian Battle'), which defied the German–Soviet Non-Aggression Pact of 1939. Building roads near Pskov, Fühmann suffered an inguinal hernia; after his recovery, he was delighted to find himself assigned to a teletype company of the air signal corps, a real soldier at last, if not on the front lines. He would see little direct action until the very end of the War. From winter 1941 to summer 1943 he was deployed at various locations in the Ukraine ('Discoveries on the Map', 'To Each His Stalingrad'); as the final German retreat began, he was transferred to Greece ('Muspilli'). Since childhood Greek mythology had fascinated him, and the confrontation with Greek reality, the juxtaposition of myth and war, would inspire much of his literary work.

He was already seeking a literary form for his experience, albeit one which mythologized war in an officially approved manner. He published his first poems in 1942; in 1944 Joseph Goebbels selected one for the weekly *Das Reich*, commenting: 'Thus writes the nameless soldier of the Eastern Front.'[6]

---

6 Gunnar Decker, *Franz Fühmann. Die Kunst des Scheiterns* (Rostock: Hinstorff Verlag, 2009), p. 82.

Yet Fühmann also made a life-changing literary discovery: the work of the Expressionist poet Georg Trakl (1887–1914). It was Trakl, he later wrote, whose dark vision and commitment to truth created the first cracks in his fascist mindset and, much later, freed him from the ideological fetters of socialism.

A brief spell of home leave in the final days of the War ('Plans in the Bramble Den') would be the last time Franz saw his father: Josef died several months later, possibly by committing suicide. Later Fühmann described a strange twist of their final encounter: coming across his book of Trakl poems, Josef commented that he had known 'poor Georgie' in the army in the First World War. This abortive conversation would haunt Franz for the rest of his life, as a fateful connection to his beloved Trakl and as an emblem of all the things he would now never be able to speak of with his father.

The scene of Fühmann's next transformation was his internment as a Soviet POW during which he was ultimately re-educated to embrace socialism. *The Jew Car* does not describe exactly how this conversion took place, though 'Rumours' describes one key moment. According to a (false) rumour, the POWs will be dispatched via 'a shot of phenol straight to the heart'. This method of execution was notoriously used in German concentration camps,

THE JEW CAR | 245so that the rumour may imply not only fear, but a
budding awareness of guilt on the part of the
soldiers. Sheer astonishment at being treated more
humanely than expected—or deserved—played a
key role in his re-education, Fühmann later wrote.
But it was through sheer chance that he was transferred from his POW camp in the Caucasus to an
anti-fascist school near Moscow. These 'Antifa'
schools were set up in the Soviet Union from 1942
onwards to re-educate German soldiers as anti-
fascist fighters and, ultimately, as builders of a post-
War socialist Germany. In his final work, *At the
Burning Abyss* (*Vor Feuerschlünden*) Fühmann
described more clearly—and critically—his 'moral
catharsis' at the Antifa school: a charismatic teacher
of Marxism–Leninism, rhetorical manipulation,
new certainties, the sense of belonging to a 'community of fate'. Above all, and above criticism, the confrontation with Auschwitz: the realization of his
own shared guilt and the desire to build a better
future. 'Even today,' he wrote, 'I recall my time at the
school as the precious fortune of a new beginning,
a process of transformation long unperceived in its
complexity . . .'[7]

On his release in 1949, Fühmann chose to settle
in the German Democratic Republic, where his

---

7 *Vor Feuerschlünden*, from *Werkausgabe in 8 Bänden* (Works
in 8 volumes, Rostock: Hinstorff Verlag, 1993), VOL. 7, p. 44.

mother and sister had been resettled. Czechoslovakia had expelled its German minority following the War, a measure which Fühmann saw as fully justified. In 1950 he married Ursula Böhm; their only child, Barbara, was born in 1952. He joined the National Democratic Party of Germany (NDPD), where he served for several years as a cultural–political functionary. One of the GDR's nominally independent parties, the NDPD was designed specifically to integrate exonerated former members of the NSDAP and the Wehrmacht, and members of the bourgeoisie. In 1954 he became an informant for the Stasi, at least on paper; apparently he declined to submit reports, and broke off contact in 1959. By that point he himself had been under surveillance for some time.

In the early 1950s Fühmann quickly came to prominence as a writer of poetry and short stories—many of which presaged *The Jew Car* in their analysis of his wartime experience—as well as numerous articles on literature and politics, often polemical, but all well within the party line. At the same time, Trakl—condemned in the GDR for 'formalism', 'anti-realism' and 'bourgeois decadence'—remained a guilty pleasure. Fühmann gradually began to chafe at the official 'realist', rationalist view of life.[8]

---

8 Ibid., p. 68.

Emboldened by the 'thaw' that followed Stalin's death, in 1956 Fühmann attempted to promote a more liberal cultural policy within the NDPD. He argued that rather than adhere to socialist realism, all writers must find their own creative methods, and proposed publishing works by such 'reactionary' writers as Franz Kafka, Jean-Paul Sartre, James Joyce and Friedrich Nietzsche. He was sharply reprimanded, cutting short his party career.[9] In the meantime, however, he had risen within the literary establishment, a member of the board of the GDR Writers' Association since 1953 and the recipient of several prestigious literary awards. From 1958 he worked full-time as a writer while remaining active in cultural politics. He also began translating poetry from the Czech and Hungarian, a lifetime vocation of more than literary importance; in some sense a kind of atonement for his Nazi past, his contacts with Czech and Hungarian writers also broadened his horizons as the GDR became increasingly stifling.

Crucially, he tried, and ultimately failed, to embrace the increasingly promoted ideal of 'working-class literature', whereby workers were encouraged to write, while non-working-class writers were supposed to 'go into the factories' to find

9 Decker, *Die Kunst des Scheiterns*, p. 134.

their subject matter. Though he would write critically of the hypocrisy and false standards which
this entailed for writers, he also experienced his
failing as a personal one.

In early 1961 Fühmann offered his publisher a
project with the working title '*Datengeschichten*'
(Date Stories), which would link stations of his
own personal development with key historical
dates. The contract for what would become *The Jew
Car* was signed on 10 August—two days before the
Berlin Wall was built. It was the beginning of a tur-
bulent decade for Fühmann. His own discontents
were growing. Yet when the left-wing West German
writers Günter Grass and Wolfdietrich Schnurre
wrote an open letter protesting the Berlin Wall, he
responded with an open letter of his own. Grass
and Schnurre argued that since West German writers were fighting injustices in the Bundesrepublik
Deutschland (BRD), including anti-communist
persecution and the presence of ex-Nazis in high
political posts, East German writers had the same
obligation to speak out against the Berlin Wall.
Fühmann called their position 'naive', arguing that
the Wall, however unpleasant, was, unlike Grass'
and Schnurre's 'well-turned phrases', an effective
blow against the ex-Nazis and anti-communists of
the BRD. 'I know the difference between red and
brown [tanks],' he wrote: 'In brown tanks I . . .
invaded the Soviet Union, and it was the people in

the red tanks who liberated me from the physical and mental slavery of Hitler's Wehrmacht[.]'[10] Here the sincerely felt personal guilt and redemption described in *The Jew Car* serves as a rhetorical trump card. (Ironically, thirty-five years later Grass caused a scandal by revealing his own youthful membership in the Waffen-SS.)

Fühmann was not alone, even among critical GDR intellectuals, in defending the Wall, believing it sadly necessary to staunch the exodus and stabilize the situation in the GDR, hopefully smoothing the way for change from within. In fact, a certain cultural and political liberalization ensued in 1963. But it was one of the last times Fühmann allowed himself to be instrumentalized as a yeasayer for the regime.

Though *The Jew Car*, published in 1962, was quite successful, he chafed at the editorial changes, ultimately publishing his original version in 1979 with the remarks cited above. My translation is based on the 1979 edition. Interestingly, if one compares the two editions, the changes prove less extensive, and less obviously ideological, than one might expect from his remarks. The most pervasive change is stylistic; in the first edition, Fühmann's

---

10 Hans-Jürgen Schmitt (ed.), *Franz Fühmann. Briefe 1950–1984. Eine Auswahl* (Rostock: Hinstorff Verlag, 1994), p. 31.

long sentences are broken up into more digestible units. This is not a trivial, nor, in a sense, an apolitical intervention: the lengthy and breathless, 'run-on' quality of Fühmann's sentences crucially shapes the narrative perspective. It vividly conveys—and subtly ironizes—the way in which the narrator is swept along by events and ideology, the tortured logic with which he attempts to make sense of things, an emotional momentum that often shades into ecstasy or hysteria. The sentence structure in the 1962 edition tones down the emotional extremes and contradictions, the immediacy and subjectivity which socialism found so threatening; it renders the narrative logic more rational—thus more compatible with socialist realism. In my translation I have done my best to honour Fühmann's stylistic choices.

In the 1960s he was already beginning to use his bully pulpit, as a functionary and prominent writer, to argue that socialist literature could flourish only if writers were 'given a much broader scope for . . . our fantasy', 'breaking with narrow conceptions of the means and possibilities of our creative work', as he wrote in an open letter to the Minister of Culture in March 1964.[11] For years to come, a huge share of his formidable rhetorical and

---

11 Ibid., p. 37.

essayistic skills was devoted to reasoning with the powers that be. The quixotic nature of the task became clear at a government plenum in December 1965, with a harsh attack from above on a wide range of prominent writers and film-makers accused of corrupting the GDR's youth with 'nihilism', 'scepticism' and 'pornography'. Only Christa Wolf (Fühmann was not present) protested her colleagues' treatment, in vain; a large number of books, films, plays and music groups were banned. In January 1966 the Writers' Association published a statement supporting the government's actions; Fühmann resigned from the board rather than sign it.

In July 1966 he revisited Rochlitz for the first time; though he never called into question the resettlement of the Sudeten Germans, he increasingly felt the loss of his homeland. He began to refer to his adopted home as 'Prussia', abandoning a project on Theodor Fontane's *Wanderings in the March of Brandenburg* due to his lack of affinity with the austere 'Prussian' culture and landscape.[12] A period of creative frustration culminated in an event that dashed hopes throughout the East Bloc. The bloody repression of the 'Prague Spring' in 1968 was especially devastating for Fühmann, with

12 Decker, *Die Kunst des Scheiterns*, p. 205.

his many contacts with Czech writers. Worst of all, his daughter Barbara, now in the eleventh grade, got into trouble at school for refusing to sign a statement supporting the Soviet invasion of Czechoslovakia. By some accounts, following further protests she was ultimately arrested and mistreated in prison.[13] Fühmann, who had increasingly struggled with alcohol problems, succumbed once again and in November finally went into rehab.

In the 1970s he delved into myth, psychology and Romanticism, especially the works of E. T. A. Hoffmann, in a search for human truths which socialism repressed, still tirelessly attempting to find a place for them within the official literary apparatus. He found one outlet for his energies in the realm of children's literature, producing remarkably playful children's books and outstanding retellings of myths and legends for young people. A literary breakthrough came in 1973 with *22 Days or Half a Life* (*22 Tage oder die Hälfte des Lebens*). Superficially the diary of a month spent in Budapest, it jettisons traditional form as a surreal kaleidoscope of dreams, memories, observations and aphorisms, ranging from apparent trivialities to reflections on Auschwitz. Increasingly, he was gaining recognition

---

13 Richter, *Ein deutsches Dichterleben*, p. 436.

in West Germany as well, with most of his works appearing in parallel West German editions (a practice which the GDR often condoned and even encouraged, as the sale of foreign rights brought hard currency into its coffers).

In 1974 he embarked on a monumental undertaking that would occupy him on and off for the rest of his life: the 'Mine Project' ('Das Bergwerk-Projekt'). Projected as a multilayered novel of over one thousand pages, it would have synthesized his exploration of myth and Romantic literature with his continued efforts to grapple with the reality of the working class: a metaphorical and literal descent into new layers of experience. Aged fifty-two, he spent several stints working in Thuringian copper and potash mines to research the novel.

For GDR intellectuals, November 1976 brought a shock comparable to that of 1968: following a few brief years of cultural thaw, the dissident singer–songwriter Wolf Biermann was unexpectedly stripped of his citizenship. Equally unexpectedly, a number of prominent writers, including Christa Wolf and Franz Fühmann, wrote an open letter to the government asking it to rethink its actions. The result was a broad wave of protest, and the state responded with repressive measures of varying harshness. At the same time, it now offered critics the option of leaving the country. The result was a mass exodus, especially of artists and intellectuals, tearing apart families and friendships and marking the beginning of the end for the GDR. Critical thinkers were suddenly faced with a wrenching choice: to leave or stay. Fühmann was placed under round-the-clock Stasi observation, and though not directly censored, he became increasingly marginalized.

Yet he never considered leaving the country, remaining true to his principle of change from within. Above all, as his Stasi file put it, he became the 'contact point and mentor' for 'hostile and oppositional forces, especially in the sphere of the so-called up-and-coming writers'.[14] A new generation of non-conformist young writers, lacking a place in the official literary scene, were withdrawing into their own unofficial one. Fühmann served as a bridge between the two, seeking publication opportunities for talents such as Uwe Kolbe and Wolfgang Hilbig who would go on to become some of Germany's most acclaimed writers. In the early 1980s he took part in what his Stasi file referred to as the 'so-called independent peace movement', and also found new inspiration in working with the mentally retarded. He managed to bring about the

---

14 Schmitt, *Briefe*, p. 597.

first and only East German editions of Sigmund Freud and Georg Trakl; his afterword for the Trakl edition spiralled into a monumental essay that intertwined his own biography and ideological transformations with reflections on Trakl's life and poetry. Published separately in 1982 under the title *At the Burning Abyss*, it would be his last major work. Though in his final years he focused once again on the 'Mine Project', he was unable to complete more than a few fragments before his death, from intestinal cancer, in 1984.

The transformation described in *The Jew Car* gained Fühmann a place in what seemed a hopeful new society. The transformations of his later life, less radical but more profound, divested him of his place even as he refused to leave.

In his brief will, from 1983, he wrote:

I am in terrible pain. The most bitter is the pain of failure: in literature and in the hope for the society that all of us once dreamt of.

I salute all my young colleagues who have chosen truth as their writing's supreme value.[15]

---

15 Decker, *Die Kunst des Scheiterns*, p. 410.

Due to his early death, and the difficulty of categorizing his complex life and oeuvre, Franz Fühmann never achieved the canonical status of, say, Christa Wolf. Yet *The Jew Car*, particularly its title story, stands as a classic of modern German short fiction and a mainstay of school and university curricula, and all his works—from essays to children's books—retain a loyal following. Nearly thirty years after his death, Fühmann has remained an inspiration, in human and artistic terms, for several generations of East and West German writers and readers. Ironically, given how consciously East German a writer he was, it is his oeuvre, with its sprawling imaginative, analytic and emotional force, that may best retain its vitality and immediacy for later generations and other cultures. Uwe Kolbe wrote in 2009:

> In . . . the literature of Fühmann's generation whose men went to the front 'for the Führer, People, Fatherland', there was hardly anyone who expressed so radically and precisely how he had become what he was, and above all how he changed. [. . .] Fühmann's almost insane endeavour, as a voracious reader and a highly productive author, was that of a universalist who could only founder upon such an ambition in his century. [. . .] What Franz

Fühmann saw as foundering, most of us
will never even achieve.[16]

---

16 Uwe Kolbe, 'Franz Fühmann: Erinnerung brennt', in *Der
Tagesspiegel*, 9 July 2009.